A Duke a Day Keeps the Doctor Away

Dukes in Danger
Book 11

Emily E K Murdoch

ARE YOU SIGNED UP FOR DRAGONBLADE'S BLOG?

You'll get the latest news and information on exclusive giveaways, exclusive excerpts, coming releases, sales, free books, cover reveals and more.

Check out our complete list of authors, too!

No spam, no junk. That's a promise!

Sign Up Here

www.dragonbladepublishing.com

Dearest Reader;

Thank you for your support of a small press. At Dragonblade Publishing, we strive to bring you the highest quality Historical Romance from some of the best authors in the business. Without your support, there is no 'us', so we sincerely hope you adore these stories and find some new favorite authors along the way.

Happy Reading!

CEO, Dragonblade Publishing

Additional Dragonblade books by Author Emily E K Murdoch

Dukes in Danger Series
Don't Judge a Duke by His Cover (Book 1)
Strike While the Duke is Hot (Book 2)
The Duke is Mightier than the Sword (Book 3)
A Duke in Time Saves Nine (Book 4)
Every Duke Has His Price (Book 5)
Put Your Best Duke Forward (Book 6)
Where There's a Duke, There's a Way (Book 7)
Curiosity Killed the Duke (Book 8)
Play With Dukes, Get Burned (Book 9)
The Best Things in Life are Dukes (Book 10)
A Duke a Day Keeps the Doctor Away (Book 11)

Twelve Days of Christmas
Twelve Drummers Drumming
Eleven Pipers Piping
Ten Lords a Leaping
Nine Ladies Dancing
Eight Maids a Milking
Seven Swans a Swimming
Six Geese a Laying
Five Gold Rings
Four Calling Birds
Three French Hens
Two Turtle Doves
A Partridge in a Pear Tree

The De Petras Saga
The Misplaced Husband (Book 1)
The Impoverished Dowry (Book 2)
The Contrary Debutante (Book 3)

The Determined Mistress (Book 4)
The Convenient Engagement (Book 5)

The Governess Bureau Series
A Governess of Great Talents (Book 1)
A Governess of Discretion (Book 2)
A Governess of Many Languages (Book 3)
A Governess of Prodigious Skill (Book 4)
A Governess of Unusual Experience (Book 5)
A Governess of Wise Years (Book 6)
A Governess of No Fear (Novella)

Never The Bride Series
Always the Bridesmaid (Book 1)
Always the Chaperone (Book 2)
Always the Courtesan (Book 3)
Always the Best Friend (Book 4)
Always the Wallflower (Book 5)
Always the Bluestocking (Book 6)
Always the Rival (Book 7)
Always the Matchmaker (Book 8)
Always the Widow (Book 9)
Always the Rebel (Book 10)
Always the Mistress (Book 11)
Always the Second Choice (Book 12)
Always the Mistletoe (Novella)
Always the Reverend (Novella)

The Lyon's Den Series
Always the Lyon Tamer

Pirates of Britannia Series
Always the High Seas

De Wolfe Pack: The Series
Whirlwind with a Wolfe

CHAPTER ONE

28 August 1811

I F HE'D PLANNED the whole thing better, Moses Warwick, Duke of Chetnole, would have arrived in daylight.

Not that he'd had much of a choice. There were only so many ships returning to England at the moment, as Moses discovered when he reached the French coast, and not all of them would take Englishmen. And of course, only one wasn't going to London.

It didn't take long to agree to the overpriced passage, nor to collect his belongings.

"Is that it?" asked Captain Toussaint.

Moses shrugged as best he could with the wound in his shoulder. "It's all I need."

Which was a lie. Moses had entered France with far more— two trunks, in fact. And a carriage. And a horse. And his health.

Still. He was leaving with his life, which he supposed he should be grateful for.

"Your family will be waiting for you at Dover, I suppose," said the captain.

Moses tried to return his smile as he leaned over the balustrade of the *Liberté*, wind whipping in the sails and rigging, his long hair falling over his eyes. The sun had set over an hour ago, and he could already see the lights of England in the distance.

Home.

Well, almost home. There was a reason he wasn't going to London, and it wasn't a reason he would explain to a French captain evidently curious about his English passenger.

Time to lie again.

"Yes," Moses said smoothly, as though speaking lies were just as easy as speaking truth. Which, by now, it was. "Yes, my wife and our three boys."

It was a falsehood he had utilized before. Where had it been?

Moses tried to think but the pain in his shoulder was growing, not fading. Wasn't a knife wound like that supposed to close after a few days?

Paris. No, Toulouse. He couldn't remember.

He had told someone he had three boys. A woman, if he recalled correctly. Someone who had been unwilling to sell him a secret about the movements of the French regiment in the nearby town. He had won her over by appealing to her conscience as a mother. As a father himself.

The pangs of guilt about lying had faded over time. Moses gave a sigh that tightened as another spurt of pain erupted from his shoulder.

"Ah, three boys!" Captain Toussaint said with a grin. "I should expect your woman will be glad for you to get back to help her keep them in order!"

Moses tried to loosen his smile. The last thing he needed was to be caught out in that most idiotic of lies. That he had a woman waiting for him. That any woman would go near him, title be damned.

"Won't be long a'fore you see them again," continued the captain in a bold, confident voice. "Waiting for you in Dover, I'll be bound."

Moses nodded rather than risk his voice.

When had he started to hate the idea of lying? When had

acting for the Crown as a spy started to become so irksome?

He couldn't point to a particular time. It had come over him so gradually, Moses could not name a date when he had realized he would rather be in England, serving his country in some other capacity, than in France lying to all and sundry.

It was time to go home. After eight months, given everything he'd been through? Definitely time.

"Captain!"

Moses jerked his head, on alert immediately thanks to the concern in the sailor's voice as he rushed up to them.

"Now then, Pierre, I'm talking to—"

"But, Captain . . ."

Moses had been perfectly prepared to eavesdrop on the conversation. Old habits died hard, and this was one he had picked up when only a boy. Curiosity and a complete inability to tell the difference between private and public—along with growing up in a castle which had more secret passageways than known corridors—had built the habit. It wasn't one he could give up.

Sadly, it was impossible to hear much of their conversation. The captain and the sailor had moved away, and the wind was blowing in the wrong direction.

Still. Moses had spent enough time around people with secrets, those sharing bad news, and individuals who did not want to be overheard to see the signs.

Something had gone wrong.

Captain Toussaint looked grave when he returned to the balustrade alongside Moses. "I apologize for that, Mr. Warwick."

Moses shrugged. At least, he meant to shrug. He caught himself just in time, preventing more agony in his shoulder. "Nothing wrong, I hope?"

"Nothing that can't be fixed," the captain said bracingly. "We make for St. Margaret's Bay."

Moses straightened. That wasn't part of the arrangement. "I paid you for—"

"I know you did, and you're not alone in your irritation Mr.

Warwick, if that is your real name," Captain Toussaint interjected testily. Gone was the cheerful, bombastic host. "I may be a Frenchman, but I'm no fool. Warwick, eh? It's a place, sir. Not a name."

Yes, he wanted to say. *Well done, sir. Warwick is indeed a place. It is also my name. That's what happens when your dukedom happens to include Warwick.*

Or at least, it had. Those pesky Wars of the Roses, they re-drew the maps in the most inconvenient of ways.

Not that he was about to reveal all this to the captain.

"St. Margaret's Bay," Moses repeated aloud.

It was a town in Kent, but that was all he could remember. It must be associated with an actual bay, or else the captain wouldn't have suggested it.

But that still did not explain—

"French ships aren't always welcome in English ports," Captain Toussaint said darkly, as though he had read Moses's thoughts. "But no matter. We make for St. Margaret's Bay, and I'm sure a gentleman like you won't have any difficulty in acquiring transportation to Dover."

"Dover?" repeated Moses blankly. *Why on earth would he want to—*

"To see your wife and your boys," said Captain Toussaint gently. There was a far too knowing look on his face for Moses's taste. "You'd better work on that story of yours, Mr. Warwick. If you wish to travel incognito, I suggest you put more thought into it."

He strode away without giving Moses a chance to respond.

As it was, Moses let the air out of his cheeks out slowly and turned back to the sea, black in the moonless night.

Well, it was not a complete disaster. The captain still had no idea who he truly was, even if he had guessed that Moses wasn't being entirely forthright. And Dover and St. Margaret's Bay couldn't be too far away from each other if the captain was able to make such a detour. Besides, it wasn't Dover he actually wanted to reach.

It was therefore with relative calm that Moses stepped onto the shore at St. Margaret's Bay, a tiny little village.

England.

He breathed in, as though he could tell the difference between French air and English air. It all tasted the same: briny, with a hint of fish. Still—he was home, sort of. Well, he was back.

"Safe travels," called the captain from the prow of the ship.

Moses raised the hand on his good arm rather than risk shouting. He wasn't sure his shoulder could take anything else.

Afterward, he supposed he should have guessed how it would be. The moment the ship weighed anchor and pulled in the gangplank, he should have known. But Moses was tired, hungry, and alone at night in a place he did not know. And he was getting old.

So when the men leapt from the shadows, he didn't even have time to grab his knife.

Not that it would have done much good. *This was a professional lot,* Moses could not help but think as he was pummeled, punched, and kicked after falling to the ground. They worked as a pack, never exerting too much energy individually, always ensuring it was impossible for him to rise from the ground.

These were men who knew precisely what they were doing.

After they trussed him up, Moses shouting at them fit to burst in the hope they would be overheard by one of the villagers, he was dropped onto the back of a dogcart.

Humiliation washed through him as the cart began to jerk.

Well, this was a fine way to return to England. The spying Duke of Chetnole, beloved by his friends, feared by his enemies . . . left on an English shore by a conniving French crew who had surely agreed with this gang to leave any gentlemen for the taking.

The bonds at his hands and feet hurt like the blazes.

But that wasn't the worst. *The question was,* Moses thought, mind spiking with pain and ribs heaving, *where were they taking him?* These were not the actions of a group of petty ruffians. No, this was far more akin to . . .

Moses's heart sank. *The Glasshand Gang.*

"I have money," he said aloud.

There was a snicker from just above him. "Not anymore, you don't."

Moses cursed himself. He was getting slow, that was his trouble. This damned shoulder. "I mean, I have more—if you release me—"

"That's what we figured, nice gentleman like y'self, fancy clothes," said a second rougher voice. "We thought—"

"Rider ho!"

The cart halted. The sudden stop made Moses roll, his shoulder protesting with every movement.

He had to think of a plan—he had to get out of here. If he truly had been caught by the Glasshand Gang, there was nothing to do but expect the worst. That, or escape.

But his knife in his belt was impossible to reach with his hands tied behind his back. Had he left a small blade in his boot? He could hardly remember, and even if he had—

"You sure?" came the question from a third voice, speaking low.

More muttering. If only Moses could have seen properly through the gloom, he might have guessed how many of them there were. How could he hope to escape these brutes if he didn't even know—

"Fine, on your head be it," muttered the same low voice. "But under protest, y'hear? This is a mistake if you ask me."

Rough hands grabbed at Moses and he bit his lip to prevent himself from crying out. The pain was excruciating, but he didn't want to give them the satisfaction.

And suddenly he was standing. The rope around his ankles was being untied, the rope around his wrists cut with a sharp knife that almost clipped his palm.

"There," said the low-voiced man who had already jumped back onto the dogcart. "Orders are orders, I suppose, but I don't see why we have to let you go."

"You don't get to—"

"I know, fine, I said on your head be it!" said the low-voiced man irritably as Moses rubbed his sore hands together, trying to take in what was happening, who was speaking, where he was. "Good luck, sir. You'll need it."

"But—"

Moses was unable to say even one word before the dogcart started forward at a faster pace than when he had been lying on it. As Moses stared in complete confusion at its receding outline, the cart was swiftly eaten up by the darkness. After a few more seconds, even the sound of the wheels and the horse's hooves had disappeared.

He was alone.

So. He was alone, in the dark, somewhere in Kent. Somewhere near St. Margaret's Bay, which was starting to sound familiar, but he wasn't even sure if it was north or south of Dover. He had no money—none at all. He'd checked all his pockets to be certain. And he'd been thoroughly beaten. There was blood dripping from his forehead, and his shoulder hurt like the blazes.

On top of all that, it was growing cold, and there was no moonlight. No one was expecting him in London. And there was no telling whether the Glasshand Gang, if that had been them, would change their minds and return for him.

That last thought prompted the only decision Moses could make. He had to move—if they came back here, he had to be gone. There was nothing else for it.

The night was overwhelming now. Struggling forward, every step feeling as though his shoulder was about to be ripped apart, Moses attempted to maintain his sense of direction.

As long as he was going forward, in a straight line . . .

But his vision was starting to become blurred, and the heat of the French day he had left behind had faded rapidly. Now he was out here, all alone, in the cool of an English breeze.

Moses stumbled. Water poured across his feet—he'd walked into a stream?

A river. Cursing the darkness for all it hid and his muddled mind for not noticing the sound of rushing water, he tried desperately to find the bank. His hands found water, then weeds, then mud.

The bank.

Coughing slightly and hating that every jerk brought his shoulder even more pain, Moses pulled himself out of the water and looked around.

Darkness, silence, in every direction.

There was a village here somewhere. Though it had been many months since he had stepped foot in England, his ability with maps had not entirely failed him . . . had it?

Moses swung his head back and forth in an agony of indecision. Left. Or right. Or straight ahead. Or behind him.

Damn it, he couldn't even recall the name of the place he was aiming for.

Clutching his shoulder, it took almost a full minute before Moses realized something his exhausted brain was shouting. His hand was warm. And wet. Not wet because of the water. Wet because of . . . something else.

Moses groaned. He was bleeding again. The stab wound in his shoulder must have opened after falling into the river—or from his beating. It was impossible to tell. The pain was the same, but the danger had now increased. The last thing he needed was an infection . . .

Glancing upward and wishing to goodness the moon would show itself, Moses made a decision.

That way.

It had no particular claim to his attention, other than it was a decision. That was what he needed. A decision. Any direction had to be better than standing here, slowly chilling.

Vision blurred and head heavy, Moses tried to put one foot in front of the other. Soon he would see a light in the distance and he could make toward it. A town, a village. Even a farmhouse would be better than nothing.

The wind grew. The Kentish moors were beautiful to look at from a carriage—God above, he'd seen them often enough. But out here at night, on his own, soaked through and bleeding copiously now, Moses knew if he did not find shelter soon, they would be the end of him.

"Damn and blast it," he muttered, as though the curses would revive him. "You should have stayed in France, you fool."

He'd not even sent word to Snee that he was returning. No one would be looking for him. No one in London—but then, the last thing he wanted was for his contacts in London to know that he had returned.

The secret had to remain his, even if he did not like it.

Exhaustion bled into his mind, and Moses staggered.

There. He blinked, sweat and river water obscuring his view. But after he'd blinked several times, Moses was certain that what he had seen had been real, even if he could not see it now. A light.

"Light," he muttered aloud, his voice hoarse.

When had he last eaten? On the ship, with Captain Toussaint?

No, his passage hadn't included a meal for the short journey over the Channel. Before that then, in France. Today? Yesterday?

Moses groaned, his shoulder burning as though it had been set ablaze. He had been certain—almost certain—he had seen a light ahead. A flicker, just dimly, but a light nonetheless. A lantern, maybe. Or the brief opening of a door—

There.

He groaned again, but this time it was with relief. A light. It was a warm light, an orangey glow. It wasn't the crisp, clear light from a beeswax candle. He was out in the middle of nowhere, far from civilization—but it meant people.

Summoning all the energy he could find, and wishing to goodness he had more, Moses forced his foot another step forward.

And tripped.

The descent to the ground was rapid, and the pain on hitting it was severe. Despite the heather, Moses's shoulder jolted agonizingly.

"Argghh!"

Despite the incaution of shouting loudly when Moses did not know if he was in danger, he could not help it. His shoulder may as well have been covered in tar and set alight, the way it felt.

Mud seeped into his ear, his cheek flat against the ground. The wind blew.

Get up, Moses thought desperately. *Get up, man! There's life out there, just before you. They could help you! Clean you up, maybe. Give you food if you're lucky.*

Yet despite the truth of what he was thinking, his body did not seem willing to obey. Or capable. It was impossible to tell which.

Exhaustion coated his bones like lead, weighing him down. The pain in his shoulder was reaching such a pitch, Moses was rather surprised he was still conscious. He'd seen lesser men collapse after receiving such a stab in the back as he had.

Figuratively and literally.

"Move," Moses moaned, as though speaking aloud would make it more likely that his body would obey. "Move, you piece of—"

He had fallen untidily, and the eye not on the ground was blearily opened in the direction of the light he had seen. Probably seen.

No, had definitely seen. There it was again, and it was moving. A lantern?

A lantern. It was being held by a figure, tall and relatively slim. A farmhand going out to check the cattle, perhaps? A man checking to see if the noise he'd heard was bandits, or robbers, or just a poor man traveling alone?

Hope swelled. If he found him—he was of no danger to anyone, surely it would be obvious by the state of him. Would this man bring him into his home? Was he saved?

"H-Help," he moaned.

The figure halted, then increased its pace toward him.

Relief, sweet relief rushed through Moses, making it easier to forget the sharp pain in his shoulder.

"Ahh," he breathed. "Help."

The lantern was almost blinding now. It did blind him for a moment as it was hastily set down on the ground beside his head.

Moses blinked. Stars were invading his vision, darkness curling at the edges of his eyes, but he thought he saw—he thought—

"Dear me," said a voice, higher than he had expected, harsh and forceful. "We have got ourselves into a state, haven't we?"

And then everything went black.

CHAPTER TWO

4 September 1811

JENNY POWELL COULD hear the difference in the bubbling from ten feet away.

"Almost," she muttered, as she closely considered the book before her. "Just a few more moments . . ."

It was a true skill. Not one she could claim was particularly useful, but Jenny had been able to do it from a young girl. Even across the kitchen, sitting up at the large table covered in crumbs and interesting scratches, she could tell when the kettle was about to boil. It had a certain pitch. She could hear it now. Her workroom was cluttered, so Jenny had to be careful as she stepped over the pair of crutches, the brace sometimes used for those who fell from trees, and the two wooden chairs haphazardly pushed from the table.

When she reached the fire, a smile crept over her face. "There."

The tincture was almost ready. Three times she had to let it cool before reheating it, and this was the second time . . .

Almost absentmindedly, Jenny pulled a pencil from the twist of curls piled high on her head and pulled out a notebook from her apron.

"Fourth of September," she wrote down carefully in a small hand. "And still no change . . ."

Despite all the promises she'd made herself to treat this one like any other patient, Jenny found her gaze flickering over to the man lying in the makeshift bed by the fire.

There he was.

She knew so little about him. Strong—she had seen the muscles when she'd ripped the shirt from his body. Tall—she'd felt his feet dragging when she had desperately hauled him to her cottage. Bold—no fearful man would have been so stupid as to attempt to pass the Westcliffe Marsh alone at that time of night.

Other than that? Jenny knew absolutely nothing about him. And the man wasn't telling. He couldn't, as he hadn't regained consciousness in all the days he'd been here.

"Where did you come from?" Jenny murmured, tapping her pencil on her notebook as she continued to stare at the man. "Who are you? What's your name?"

They were not questions she could answer. Oh, there were certain things she could deduce. He had hands which had not seen work for years, then suddenly seen harshness. That was clear from the calluses on his hands.

He was a well-educated man. There was no denying it—the shirt she'd unceremoniously ripped to tatters had been made of fine linen. The clean parts had made wonderful bandages.

And he was dangerous.

Jenny swallowed as her pencil abruptly halted tapping.

Yes, dangerous. Safe, calm, regular men did not wander around with knife wounds in their backs.

Still, she had stitched him up, Jenny thought dryly as she lifted the tincture off the fire to let it rest. The fever which set in had been expected, and she had done her best to nurse him through it.

She'd half hoped he would mutter something during the worst parts of his illness, but he had not. Well, he had, but nothing comprehensible. Screams, mostly.

"And now your fever's broken. It's been broken for over a day," Jenny said, stepping forward toward her patient, "and you haven't woken."

That in itself was slightly concerning. She'd never known for sleep to remain this long after a fever—but then, the shoulder was still healing. It was difficult to tell precisely how long he would remain asleep.

Ignoring all her instincts, Jenny sat gently down beside the man.

And he was handsome.

Utter foolishness, she thought resolutely. *Looks are just a chance of fate—and what Society deemed impressive at the time! Button noses were once fashionable, and now . . .*

Now this was. Oh, there was no point denying it. Jenny would never permit a man to be bold enough to get this close were he awake, but that didn't mean she couldn't just for a moment examine this one.

A dark, proud brow, even in sleep. Long hair which she had untidily clipped short, it had been getting so in the way of her work. Broad shoulders, even with the injury. And a look . . .

Jenny swallowed. A look of kindness.

But that couldn't be true. He was a dangerous man, a ruffian, undoubtedly involved in something nefarious. Why else would he have been out on Westcliffe Marsh, collapsed with a stab wound in his shoulder?

"You are a mystery," Jenny whispered, brushing her hand over his hair and feeling his forehead. No fever. "My mystery man."

She sat, just for a moment, in his presence. It was strange. Even though she knew he was no good, there was something incredibly . . . well, calming about the man.

Jenny shook herself. "Utter foolishness."

Rising to her feet, she stepped over to the table and lifted the lid of the pot. The smell hit her immediately. Perfect. Ready to go back on the fire. Another heat through—

"F-Foolishness?"

Jenny froze, lid in hand. *Did she just hear . . .*

"Foolish . . . where the hell . . .?"

Slowly turning on her toes, Jenny looked over at the pallet she'd made days ago.

He had woken up.

Well, sort of. Jenny did not have to be an expert to spot the hazy look in his eyes, the confused way the man dragged his hand through his hair, the astonished look when he found his hair to be significantly shorter than he had expected.

The man had been asleep, unconscious, and in a fever for over a week. No wonder he was a little disoriented.

Everything Jenny knew slipped into place, moving her to instinct rather than thought.

"Do you know where you are?" she said slowly, putting the lid down and starting to approach him.

The man was trying to sit up, but he was obviously weak after remaining still for so long. "I-I . . . I . . ."

"Stay calm, and stay still," Jenny said firmly, but she hoped not unkindly.

She had reached him now. Seating herself in the chair where she had spent the last few evenings knitting and watching for any sign of the man waking, Jenny peered deep into his eyes.

Her stomach jolted.

Now that wasn't supposed to be the reaction to examining a sick person . . .

"What do you want?" the man said, veering away as though she intended to hurt him.

Which, Jenny recalled, he could not know. For all he knew, she *was* someone who intended to hurt him. Who knew what sort of people he had been running from? They certainly didn't have any qualms about stabbing a man.

"Who are you?" Jenny asked, lifting a hand to his forehead and trying to appear trustworthy.

Yes, she was right before. The fever had completely broken.

He felt fine, actually. Hearty. There was a warmth in him you only found in a well person. The boiling, fizzing heat of the fever had gone.

"My name is Moses," said the man stiffly, as though he was giving her a great favor by answering. "And you still haven't given me your name."

"You can call me Powell," said Jenny softly, withdrawing her hand and sitting back in her chair.

Well, he spoke English. You never could tell, living so close to the coast. This wouldn't be the first time a poor man had been washed up onto the shore and then brought to her, not speaking a word of English.

And he spoke it well. There was an imperiousness about him that only came with breeding. This was a man who should be dining with friends, hunting, losing money at cards.

So what was he doing here in her workroom?

"What's the last thing you remember?" Jenny asked softly.

Kindness and softness, that was what she had to remember. It was the hardest part. Mixing the tinctures and salves, knowing how to set a broken bone, recognizing when a woman was truly in labor or just experiencing pains . . . that was easy.

It was the gentleness she had always struggled with.

Jenny set her jaw. Not because she wasn't gentle, but because people made it so difficult.

"Remember?" the man asked blankly.

A flicker of fear. She had known a fever to take memory before. At least, she had read about it.

Her gaze snapped over to her precious library.

She called it a library. Really it was just three shelves of books she had managed to buy over the years, and there weren't many at that. But still. It was far more knowledge than she had ever expected to accumulate. She was almost certain she had read about just this sort of thing before.

"I . . . I'm not sure what I can remember," the man said warily.

Jenny snorted. There was such deception in the man's face, she didn't need to know a thing about him to say, "You're lying."

"Moses" bristled, then drew a quick intake of breath. "How dare you—"

"I dare because this is my home, and you are the guest here," said Jenny matter-of-factly, ignoring his outraged expression to tilt the man to the left. "Let me look."

"Woman, what are you—"

"Jenny Powell will do," Jenny said evenly.

You have to stay calm when doing this. Over the years, she had learned to tell which patients would prove troublesome, and which would happily accept the cod liver oil without audible complaint.

The important thing was not to notice the spark of heat tingling along her fingers as she touched him.

He was just a patient, Jenny tried to tell herself, ignoring the shuddering jolt in her stomach as she maintained the contact between her and this Moses.

It wasn't anything special. She didn't feel something she had never felt before.

She focused on the wound. It was still horrendous to look at. Jagged, made by a knife, if she were to guess, that had a rough edge rather than a clean one. The injury had looked awful when she'd first brought the man inside. A gaping open wound, red irritated skin all around it, infection already setting in.

If she hadn't already had a few things made up and put by, she doubted he'd be awake now. Or ever.

"It doesn't hurt."

Jenny's spirit soared at the man's soft words.

This was why she did what she did. The surprise in the man's voice, this Moses, if that was his real name. That was why she worked so hard, scrimped and saved for the best medicines, determinedly stayed in East Langdon even when she knew, at times, she was not welcome.

Because it would lead to this. A person being healed.

Jenny allowed the man to settle back in the bedlinens and permitted herself a small smile. "I'm glad."

"I thought, for a while . . . on the ship . . ."

She waited. Experience—or rather, her own mistakes—had taught her that jumping in to interrupt someone as they were trying to recall what had happened before a fever never ended well. It was best just to be silent. Let the memories surface slowly.

"I was on a ship," said the man calling himself Moses. "From . . . from somewhere. Back to England, I wanted to get back to England."

Jenny nodded and waited.

Moses's eyes were flicking left and right, as though searching for the answers in her room. "What is this place?"

Looking around her, Jenny beamed. It was rather unusual, even she would admit that.

When she had moved into West Cottage, she hadn't intended to do much entertaining. There hadn't been much point. She had no acquaintance in the village, and little interest in creating one.

And so the drawing room, such as it was, had felt rather immaterial. It was south facing, perfect for capturing the sunshine all year round. And most unusually, because it was long rather than wide, it had two fireplaces—one she used for creating medicines and tinctures, and one to keep herself and her patients warm.

Little remained of the original furnishings. The sofa had gone, though she'd kept two armchairs which she used for reading and keeping patients comfortable. The large kitchen table had been brought in here, ideal for chopping up ingredients and, God forbid she ever had to do it, patients in need of amputation.

Herbs and spices hung from the ceiling. There were two large cupboards and a smaller dresser, all full of jars and tins and tubs. A blanket box by the wall was full of bed linens and strips of linen from old sheets, perfect for wounds.

The whole effect must be rather astonishing for someone who didn't spend almost all their waking time within it.

"This is the workroom," she said softly.

Moses nodded, as though he understood. "I . . . I see."

"And now I need to see," Jenny said decisively, turning back to him. "You say your first name is Moses—but what about your surname?"

There was no mistaking that look. She had seen it before in a pair of louts she had aided in exchange for them returning the sheep they had stolen over the way.

This man was hiding from the law.

The thought was so sharp, so insistent, it made Jenny catch her breath.

She had a criminal under her roof. Well, it wouldn't be the first time, nor the last, she supposed. But still. It put her in a rather dangerous situation. One she would not have chosen, if she could.

But then the man's brow settled, and a smile he clearly thought was charming slipped across his face. "Moses Warwick."

Jenny worked hard not to roll her eyes. "Indeed?"

Why did they always think that choosing something so obvious would make them look innocent? Warwick indeed. He may as well have said Kent!

The trouble was, that smile was remarkably thawing. She was rising in temperature, and as Jenny looked back at the man, her heart skipped a beat.

This was intolerable! She was not about to allow herself to be taken in by a man just because he could smile, Jenny thought. He was almost certainly a criminal, and a liar to boot! No, all she had to do was get him well enough to talk, and the ruffian could be on his way. Out of her workroom, and out of her life.

"Where am I?" Mr. Warwick—for want of a better name—asked.

Jenny's attention focused. There was a tired slurring of the words. The man was exhausted, the sleep he'd had these last days insufficient to provide both healing and clarity of mind.

Well, there was a remedy for that.

Rising to her feet and stepping to one of her cupboards, she said, "I was going to ask you if you could recall."

"I have no memory of being brought here," he said slowly.

Jenny nodded as she searched along the shelves. *It had been here yesterday* . . . "You were found."

"Found?"

She didn't need to say that she was the one who had found him. That information, if she ever needed to share it, could be given another day.

"Found and brought here," Jenny said, reaching into the depths of the cupboard. Her fingers closed around a small square jar. *There it was.*

"I-I don't remember . . . I thought I was—but I couldn't have been. Why wouldn't I go to London?"

Jenny turned around as a rush of sympathy overtook her. She could hardly imagine what it must be like. Waking up in a strange place with an injury that could have killed him. Naked from the waist up, unexpectedly. A strange woman meandering about what appeared to be an apothecary, and his memory hazy.

A shiver curled down her spine. It must be terrifying.

"I know this must all be very confusing," she said quietly.

Mr. Warwick was trying to sit up again, but he simply didn't have the strength. Jenny could see the panic building in him and knew beyond a shadow of a doubt that if he struggled, all the healing she had managed to achieve in his shoulder would be for naught.

She had to give him this draught as soon as possible.

"Lie back," Jenny said, pouring a bit from the jar into a glass and adding some light ale before stepping back to him. "Please, calm yourself."

"I don't know how I got here—I don't know why I wasn't in London!" the man said wretchedly. "What else don't I remember?"

Jenny swallowed. She'd never had a case quite like this. She had been proud of herself for cleaning the wound so well, and she'd kept the man alive, which was more than she could say for some people in her line of work.

But this? Memory? Understanding how the mind worked was a challenge at the best of times. She frequently wondered why men made the decisions they did even when they had full possession of their faculties.

The day-to-day confusions of everyday men, however, were nothing to the effects a week-long fever on an already weak individual.

"Drink this a moment, then we can talk," she said soothingly.

For a moment, she thought Mr. Warwick would refuse. He knew nothing of her save for her name. And that could be a lie.

It wasn't. Not completely. But it could have been.

And she knew nothing of him. Jenny's curiosity had been piqued the moment she had thought she'd heard the cry. Taking her lantern and going looking for the man had been instinct. Second nature. Something she had done simply because it was the right thing to do.

She had questioned that just a little as she had struggled to carry the heavy man into her workroom. But still, it was the right thing.

But other than that, she knew nothing. What if, once this "Mr. Warwick" gained his strength, he hurt her? Attacked her? Stole from her, perhaps? There were many valuable things she possessed in this room alone.

For a heartbeat, Jenny looked down into Mr. Warwick's eyes and saw the same fear, the same uncertainty.

They had to trust each other. What else could they do?

"Drink," Jenny said softly, bringing the glass to his lips.

Mr. Warwick obeyed even as he kept his eyes on her. Jenny ignored the stir in her stomach as he did so with those questioning eyes. When it was all gone, she lifted the glass from his mouth and placed it upon the table beside her.

"Are you certain your name is Warwick?" Her gentle question did not, unfortunately, receive a gentle answer.

The man immediately frowned, anger in his expression. "Why would you doubt me?"

"You recall so little about yourself and your past," Jenny said with a shrug, ignoring how the man's struggles to sit up had caused the coverlet to slip to his waist. Revealing his naked chest.

She was not going to look. It was just a body. Just a strong, broad chest. Just a muscular chest with dark hair that trailed—

"I know my own name," said Mr. Warwick resolutely.

Jenny raised an eyebrow. "Warwick? Really?"

The man's eyes were shifting in and out of focus. "I—why does no one . . . I feel strange."

Ah, so it was starting to work then. Good.

But just as Jenny was feeling satisfied with a job well done, all hell broke loose. Moses Warwick lunged, his hands grasping her arms, and she cried out as he pulled her toward him.

"The ale—what did you give me? Woman, you've poisoned me!"

"I haven't—it's not—" Jenny's mind was racing, heart thundering.

Mr. Warwick did not let go. "You've killed—I'm . . . not sleepy . . ."

It was all over in a matter of seconds. Though her pulse still thumped rapidly and fear had risen into her throat, Jenny was able to prize the man's hands from her as the concoction overwhelmed him, and he fell back into the camp bed, eyes closed.

Jenny panted into the silence, hardly able to believe what had just happened. "Right."

Now all she had to do was wait for him to wake up again and hope he didn't murder her in her bed.

CHAPTER THREE

6 September 1811

THE JOURNEY BETWEEN waking and sleeping, Moses was discovering, was far more of a challenge than he had expected.

It was the grogginess. That was it. The feeling his head had been sat on by a large elephant. The sense he had to surface from very deep underwater. The confusion about why he couldn't move his legs . . .

Wait. He couldn't move his legs?

Moses opened his eyes.

The ceiling above him was barely a ceiling. It appeared to be more like a repository for an upside-down garden. There were more plants up there than he would know what to do with. Herbs, by the look of it, but also a few he would have called weeds. Some, he did not recognize at all.

It was not a ceiling he knew.

Moses would have expected that thought to cause panic, but for some reason, it didn't. While being entirely strange, that ceiling was also somehow strangely familiar. As though he had seen it before, but not for long. Almost as if—

"This is the workroom."

Moses blinked. *Workroom?*

Though his shoulder felt stiff and difficult to move, he could sit up. The pillow behind him was particularly plumped, allowing him to see more of the room.

There was a large wooden table in one corner, covered in scales and knives and some sort of basket filled with what looked like linen. Around the table were three wooden chairs. Upon one of those wooden chairs . . .

Moses swallowed.

It was all coming back to him now. The woman seated on that chair, not yet aware he had woken, was carefully reading something in a large, leatherbound book.

"Woman, what are you—"

"Jenny Powell will do."

Jenny Powell. The name surfaced in Moses's mind as though he had been reaching for it. Perhaps he had. It had been her who had given him that ale, the ale which had made him fall sleep so quickly.

He had lunged at her, as he recalled. Moses winced, not only at the memory of the pain that had jolted through his shoulder at the time, but at his ill manners.

The woman had clearly been trying to help. The doctor must have asked her to give it to him, and he had been most uncouth in his response. An apology would be needed at some point.

But that could wait. First—

Moses grimaced in anticipation as he reached around to his shoulder, expecting to feel pain and discomfort.

His eyes widened.

The cut was gone. Well, not gone. But healed almost completely. His fingers scraped along the scar which was forming. There was no real pain there at all. Stiffness, yes, but that had surely come from lying down here for . . .

How long?

"Ah. You're awake."

Moses froze, then relaxed. He needed her help, whatever she

could give. He could hardly make his way to London like this.

Because that was where he was going, wasn't it? London?

"Jenny Powell," he said aloud.

Miss Powell glanced over. "Well remembered. Do you recall anything else?"

Moses hesitated.

It was coming back to him now. Not just the strange interaction he had shared with the woman when he had first come round in this strange place, but more than that. His life, who he was. What he had been doing in France, and . . .

And *not* why he had returned.

Frowning, Moses tried to reach into the depths of his mind, but either his brain would not or could not retrieve that particular information.

"I recall quite a bit," he said warily to the woman.

He was hardly going to admit who he was—and what he had been doing in France—was he? No, he would keep that information to himself. No one, particularly not a young woman, needed to hear that information.

"I have to apologize," said Miss Powell awkwardly, rising and smoothing her skirt.

Moses's frown softened.

Well, if he was going to have to recuperate here in this odd workroom, he couldn't think of a more pleasant person to do it with. This Miss Powell—no, it would surely be Mrs. Powell, an unmarried woman wouldn't be here alone—would be his companion.

And what a companion.

Moses sat up straighter and was suddenly conscious that he was half naked and speaking with a beautiful woman. Tall, lithe, with light brown hair piled on top of her head which held—

Moses blinked. *Was that—it couldn't be a pencil, could it?*

Well, she may be a little eccentric, but she was going to be an interesting companion to heal for. *With,* Moses corrected swiftly. *Her husband probably wouldn't thank you for looking at her like that, my lad. Better you concentrate on getting your strength up.*

"I am sorry I frightened you," said Mrs. Powell, stepping toward him. "Giving you that ale with the powder to make you sleep."

Moses shrugged and was delighted to discover it did not hurt to do so. "I understand now, but at the time I thought—"

"You thought I was attempting to kill you," said Mrs. Powell succinctly as she sat beside him. "What an interesting life you must have led."

Moses tried to smile. *Ah, hell. A clever one.*

They were always the worst. It was so much easier to keep a woman at arm's length if she was dim, not interested in actual conversation but just being a duchess.

A duchess—wait. Had he told her he was a duke?

Moses tried to review his memories, all they had discussed when he had last awoken, but parts were hazy, and he wasn't too sure how much he had said. But she had not called him "Your Grace," had she?

"Will you forgive me, Mr. Warwick?" Mrs. Powell asked formally.

He relaxed into the bedlinens. *He hadn't given his true identity—that was a relief.*

"Of course," he said magnanimously. "I am sure yesterday you merely wished to—"

"It was two days ago, actually," said Mrs. Powell with a wry look. "I think it was mixed a little stronger than intended."

She was a good wife, Moses thought with a sinking heart. That would have been the perfect opportunity to criticize her husband's mixing error, as surely many spouses would have done. Yet she was loyal. A shame she was already taken.

"Thank you for caring for me," Moses said stiffly.

"My pleasure," she said quietly. "Cigar?"

He shook his head. "Hate the stuff."

That was it. Maintain distance. It was what he usually did whenever he came into contact with anyone, so it was not difficult to slip back into the routine. Even if it was a shame with a woman this pretty.

And he was grateful. God only knew what would have happened to him if he had been left out there in the midnight cold Kentish countryside. Moses didn't like to think. His shoulder certainly wouldn't have been this healed, to begin with.

The trouble was, he had no money to give her or her husband.

At least Moses could now remember why. That damned Glasshand Gang, was no one ever going to bring them to justice?

But it rather complicated things here, did it not? His jacket was gone and his shirt too, so the Powells must know he had no coin. The question was why they were still caring for him as though he could pay them for their ministrations?

There was nothing for it. Moses took a deep breath and resigned himself to losing time with this beautiful woman. He would have to ask for her husband.

"You have done me a great service, and I am grateful—and will be able to pay, once I have returned home," Moses said proudly. "Now, I must discuss a few things with the doctor."

Firstly, just how long he had been here, he thought ominously. And secondly, whether he had muttered anything incriminating in his sleep.

The last thing he needed was for the Powells to know what he had been up to.

"Yes, I suppose that is the right thing to do," said Mrs. Powell, a smile tweaking the corners of her mouth. "You were gravely injured."

"I do not know what I would have done if I had not been found," Moses admitted.

It was a difficult thing to admit. Chetnoles were not known for their ability to cooperate. His father, and his father before him, had been dukes who preferred to struggle alone, and Moses was conscious of the fact that he was no different.

Oh, he had friends. At least, people he liked and whose company he tolerated. Though he was not sure, now he came to think about it, whether they would consider him a friend. It was a startling thought—one he did not like.

He would have to consider it more deeply later.

"It was difficult to get you inside," Mrs. Powell was saying. "You are much heavier—I mean stronger—than you look."

Moses was gratified to see pink in her cheeks.

It was pleasant to know he still had a bit of appeal, even as an invalid! If he could just forget that she was married to the doctor who had saved his life, perhaps this could be . . .

But no. He was not that sort of man.

He may have no interest in marrying and settling down, but that did not mean he didn't respect the boundaries of those who did. When a man found a woman he wished to devote the rest of his life to, Moses was not going to be the one who came between them.

Even if Mrs. Powell was delightful.

"The doctor," Moses said firmly. *He mustn't forget the man of the house!* "I must see him."

There was a twinkle in the woman's eye. "Yes, the doctor is in."

Shifting onto his elbows, Moses looked around the workroom. It was prodigiously large, larger than he had expected. Some parts were hidden by screens or cabinets or shelves.

But for the life of him, he couldn't see a doctor.

"Where?" said Moses in confusion. "I don't see him."

"You don't?" Mrs. Powell asked lightly.

She seemed almost amused by his inability to spot the doctor. Concern flashed in Moses's stomach. *Why couldn't he see the doctor? Where in God's name was he?*

"No, I can't see the doctor at all."

"How interesting," said Mrs. Powell, voice quiet. "The doctor's right in front of you."

Fear gripped Moses. He tried to sit up straighter, eyes darting about the place.

Was it possible—dear God, could he have had some sort of fever that affected his vision? Oh, if he lost his eyesight, he would have to learn to do so much unaided! It would be strange, frightening, stepping into the unknown!

"I-I think I'm going blind," Moses croaked.

He hated how the fear he felt moved immediately into his voice, but he could not help it. He was weak, weary, alone, and without funds, and now he was losing his sight?

Mrs. Powell shook her head. "I think you're losing your reason, too."

Reason? What on earth was she going on about?

"This is not the time for japes," Moses snapped. "Where is the doctor? Where is he?"

He ceased hunting about the workroom for the missing man, and instead glared at the woman beside him.

Moses's stomach lurched. She was smiling, and the smile unlocked an even greater level of beauty in her than he had realized. Goodness, she was stunning. What was she doing here, married to a country doctor in the middle of nowhere?

"She," Mrs. Powell said quietly, "is sitting next to you."

For a moment, he just stared. Moses allowed the words to linger in his mind, to seep gently in, to echo around his head.

"Where is the doctor? Where is he?"

"She is sitting next to you."

It was a foolish joke—one in particularly poor taste, considering how unwell he had been. Why didn't she just call her husband and get him in here?

"There is no need to be so facetious," he snapped.

"And there is no need for you to be so rude," Mrs. Powell returned.

There was a grit in her voice he had not heard before. She was looking at him boldly, no fear in her eyes, no natural reticence in her expression.

If this were any other situation, Moses may find the look alluring. In this moment, it was simply maddening.

"Mrs. Powell, I have no wish to be rude—"

"Why do I feel you are going to continue being so anyway?" she asked quietly.

Moses ignored her. The woman was being idiotic, and he had to speak plainly. "Women are not doctors. They simply aren't—it's the way of the world. There are no woman doctors, and I have been most seriously ill. You may not understand—"

"I think you'd be surprised at how little I don't understand," Mrs. Powell said, firmness in her tone. "I think you'd be surprised at what you don't understand, too, Mr. Warwick."

Moses almost flinched at the awkward sound of his informal name but did not press it. He was Moses Warwick, even if he was also the Duke of Chetnole. She did not know that—though perhaps if she did, she would not be quite so discourteous.

"I doubt that very much, Mrs. Powell," he said sardonically. "And once your husband is here, I am sure he will want to hear about how disobliging you have been to one of his patients."

And that was when he saw it. Fire—he could have sworn it was actual fire—flaring in the woman's eyes.

Dear God, she was magnificent.

"How dare you talk to me like that in my own workroom!" she demanded fiercely. "The cheek! You think you are the sum total of all knowledge in the world? You think anything unfamiliar to you must be untrue?"

"I do not have the energy to debate semantics with you," Moses said wearily. *God's teeth, but she was a gorgon.* "I want to speak to your husband."

"Oh, you do?"

Moses watched, astounded, as Mrs. Powell rose and placed her hands on her hips.

Really, she was dazzling. In another world, in another life, this conversation could have been very different, Moses could not help but think. If he had met her before she'd married this Doctor Powell, whom he seemed destined never to meet . . . well, he would certainly have tasted those lips, known what it was to hold those hands, to feel those hips underneath him—

"—and you're not even listening to me!"

Moses blinked, then shook his head as though ridding water from his ears. Mrs. Powell was examining him with great ire, and he hardly knew how to respond.

After all, he *hadn't* been listening.

"I have been ill," he said defensively.

"I well know that," said Mrs. Powell with a roll of her eyes. "Who do you think has been taking care of you?"

"Your nursing, I am sure, was very—"

"I am the doctor, you idiot," said Mrs. Powell tightly. "I've taken care of you for weeks, since the moment you—"

"Weeks?" Moses repeated faintly.

No. That couldn't be right. He had been here only a few days, surely. There was no growth of beard, no sense of time passing. *But then,* Moses thought agitatedly, *he had thought their last conversation had been yesterday, and that had been two days ago. Was it possible, when he had been in the depths of his fever . . .*

How long had he actually been here?

"Just over a week," said Mrs. Powell decidedly. "It was the twenty-eighth of August when I found you, and it's the sixth of September now."

The sixth of September?

Moses's mind raced. It did not seem possible, yet he had heard that when a man was truly sick, his sense of time could sometimes be a tad . . . lacking, for want of a better word. Was it possible he had been here for so long at the mercy of this woman and her husband, who apparently disliked patients so much that he refused to see them when they were conscious?

Mrs. Powell was still standing beside the makeshift bed he was lying on, her hands still on her hips. "Now do you believe me?"

"I . . . I . . ." *Damn it,* thought Moses bitterly. *I'm a step behind here. I hate being a step behind.* "I can believe I have been here a great deal longer than I expected—"

"I apologize, by the way, if I nicked you while shaving you," said Mrs. Powell with a gleam in her eye. "I'm unaccustomed to keeping a man clean shaven, but I thought it would help with your recovery."

Moses glared. "Thank you."

It was most infuriating, lying here on this bed like a child. If he had his health, he'd be standing tall, taller even than her. She'd soon see what sort of a man she was crossing swords with—metaphorically, naturally—and she'd soon listen to reason. As it was . . .

"Your husband, dear lady," Moses said wearily. "I just want to talk to him."

"I have no husband," said the inexplicable Mrs. Powell.

Now that was a surprise. Yet now he came to think about it, had she ever actually said that she was married? How had she given her name—Mrs. Powell?

"My name is Moses. And you still haven't given me your name."

"You can call me Powell."

Moses's heart sank. *Ah. Okay, fine. Not a husband.* "I'll talk to your brother, then."

Miss Powell's face fell, and her hands slipped to her sides. "Why on earth would you want to do that?"

Perhaps he was more tired from the exertion of healing than he thought, Moses considered as he rubbed his temple. It all seemed rather obvious to him.

"I cannot believe I am saying this, again," he said testily, "but I want to see the doctor. Husband, brother, I don't care what he is to you, but—"

"I am the doctor, Mr. Warwick," Miss Powell said slowly, her voice firm and steady. "I am the one who mixes the tinctures and sets bones. I'm the one with the books and the learning. I know how to stop a wound from bleeding and how to keep it clean. Me. I'm the doctor. I'm the one who cared for you, and I'm the one who is losing patience."

She wasn't the only one. Moses sighed, shaking his head.

It was sad, really. But he wouldn't allow himself to get swept up in whatever game Miss Powell was playing. She may find comfort in the act of playing at doctor, but he wanted a true medical man to step forward and take a look at his shoulder.

"Miss Powell—"

"You may call me Doctor Powell," she said with a dangerous glint in her eye.

Moses looked resolutely back. "Now that, I will never do."

CHAPTER FOUR

10 September 1811

THIS TIME, JENNY almost walloped him with a wooden spoon. "What the—Mr. Warwick!"

At least this time he had the good manners to look a little sheepish. "I just—"

"I don't care what you were just about to do, Mr. Warwick," said Jenny sternly, waving her wooden spoon imperiously. "I told you, stay out of my way!"

It shouldn't be that difficult. Jenny had never discovered a man with such a penchant for wandering about. It was criminal!

She supposed it didn't help that she was unaccustomed to having anyone in the workroom with her for any significant length of time.

Oh, people visited. Those who wanted their coughs and colds seen to. Those who were nervous about a boil, or confused about a rash that always came up whenever they strode through a particular field.

But they were in her workshop for the small amount of time it took her to sort out the specific ailment, and then they were gone. Even then, they sat carefully in the armchair she pointed them to. They didn't go wandering about, getting under her feet and constantly causing her to crash into them.

Jenny tried to put the thought of crashing into Mr. Warwick from her mind. He was even taller than she had predicted, and despite his illness, he still had a great deal of strength. The first three times she had careered into him, turning around quickly without thinking there could possibly be a man standing behind her, Jenny had been astonished at just how . . . well, solid he had been.

After that, it had simply been annoying.

"I don't want to sit, though," Mr. Warwick said helplessly, shrugging his shoulder. Jenny spotted that one was still held lower than the other. "Just sitting around all day—"

"Isn't that what you gentlemen do?" Jenny shot back, irritation spilling over into accidental—*fine, not entirely accidental*—rudeness.

She was rewarded by a flare of exasperation in Mr. Warwick's eyes. She watched him struggle with it, watched him wish to say something cutting, and watched him swallow it.

He was a controlled man. It was difficult not to be at least a little impressed by such a man who wished to shout yet still held his tongue. It was far more than most men could manage.

"Many gentlemen do, I suppose," Mr. Warwick conceded. "But I am not the sort of man who likes to lounge about the place. I like to be busy. Useful."

His glare was pointed.

Jenny ignored it. They had already had this conversation and she wasn't about to have it again. Mr. Warwick's assertion that he could do almost everything she did—and better—was growing wearing.

Besides, he wasn't even back to full strength. She could see the beaded sweat on his brow. All this walking about, even in her workroom, was tiring him out.

Jenny placed a hand on his arm and tried to ignore what shot through her. "Mr. Warwick, you need to rest."

"What would you know?" he remarked testily.

She was not going to have this argument again.

Honestly, he was the most trying patient she had ever had, and that included Mr. Saunders who had been most frustrating at his wife's first birth. He'd been even more frustrating when he himself had been sick. Useless man.

But Mr. Warwick could now claim the top spot, Jenny thought bleakly, adjusting her internal ranking of irritating patients.

Number three, her own father. The less said about him, the better.

Number two, Mr. Saunders.

And number one, Mr. Warwick. Or whatever his real name was.

"I am not going to argue with you again about whether I am a doctor or not," Jenny said as mildly as possible. "I wouldn't even need to be a doctor to see the way you are holding that shoulder. You're weak."

Mr. Warwick bristled. "I am most certainly not—"

"Your body is weak, Mr. Warwick," Jenny said jadedly. *Honestly, did every man have to be so vain?* "You need to recover. I can see you're tired, and if you keep prowling about my workroom like a caged lion, you'll set your recovery back even further."

She watched him hesitate, biting the corner of his lip as he considered. Those lips—

"And worse," Jenny said, mostly to distract herself rather than to say anything meaningful. "If you keep getting in my way, I'm going to wallop you."

She met his stern look with one just as firm and tried to ignore the swooping sensation in her stomach.

It was strange, having anyone around this much. Jenny had lived quite happily for almost three years in West Cottage without a single soul. She could do for herself, had done now for quite some time. Why would she even need a maid?

Solitude was something she had craved at first. Now it was such a habit, she was rather astonished she hadn't walloped Mr. Warwick already just for being present. Not that it would be very kind.

Still. He could stop getting in her way.

Mr. Warwick was looking at her curiously. "You wouldn't."

"Wallop you for once again getting in my way so I couldn't return a salve to the fire and would therefore have to start all over again?" Jenny stuck out her chin. "Watch me."

For a moment they just stared at each other. He stood, his arm now cradled in the other in an attempt to relieve the pressure on his sore shoulder. She stood, wooden spoon in one hand and the other placed on her hip.

Jenny had never competed in a staring match. It was the sort of thing her brother would do and she would be punished for, so she never did.

Perhaps she should have done. It would have been excellent practice.

Eventually Mr. Warwick hung his head. "I do not mean to get in the way."

"Prove it by sitting yourself down for more than ten minutes together," said Jenny wearily. "I have to get this salve finished, and I'm tired."

It was foolish of her to admit such weakness, but she couldn't help it. There was something so . . . so intense about having someone about her all the time.

Jenny was not a particularly unsociable person. When she had been more in Society, she had not minded spending time with those she already liked, in moderation.

But that was the key. *Moderation.* Even when she had lived at home, Jenny had known she was fatigued by company more than others. She liked solitude. She liked the quiet.

Living here alone in West Cottage, Jenny had settled happily into her own routine that allowed her to do whatever, whenever, however she wanted. It was glorious. After living under someone else's roof for so long and living by their rules, living alone was heaven.

Mr. Warwick grunted rather than replied and settled into the armchair with what could have been politely called ill grace.

Jenny sighed, relief dancing through her bones. *There. A little quiet, and she could concentrate on—*

"What are you making?"

She had only just turned back to the kitchen table. That was how long he was able to remain silent?

Though she hadn't actually asked him to be quiet as well as out of the way. Perhaps she should have done.

Jenny tried to ignore it, but the prickling irritation she felt whenever Mr. Warwick was speaking once again returned. After all that nonsense he had given her about not being a doctor, after refusing to call her a doctor the days he had been awake . . .

"You may call me Doctor Powell."

"Now that, I will never do."

And he dared to ask her what she was making!

"A salve," Jenny said shortly.

She picked up her knife and sighed. Well, the batch she had been working on was ruined. She hadn't returned it to the fire soon enough. She would have to start again. Thankfully, Mrs. Guernsey had paid her in a particularly fine bunch of herbs, and if she recalled correctly, there was some lavender in that. She should have enough to—

"What for?"

Jenny's fingers tightened around the sprigs of lavender. One broke.

She shouldn't be permitting him to get to her like this. It was ridiculous! Just because she liked her own company, that did not mean she was incapable of enjoying someone else's.

At least, that was what she had thought before Mr. Warwick had invaded her home.

That isn't fair, a quiet voice from the back of her mind pointed out. *You were the one who brought him here. He didn't ask to be here.*

He would have died if I had left him out there! Jenny shot back at the irritating voice.

That's as may be, replied the voice smugly. *But he didn't, did he?*

"I said—"

"I heard what you said," Jenny bit back. Truly, he was most provoking. "I don't know why you're asking me. Why not ask the doctor you believe is here somewhere?"

It was harsh, but she was swiftly losing her patience with this man who would happily accept her medical ministrations, then deny she could possibly have the talent for it.

"You could just throw me out," came Mr. Warwick's voice. It was mild, as though he barely cared one way or the other. "I'm sure I am strong enough to—"

Jenny snorted. "You wouldn't make it a mile from East Langdon."

And that, she thought as she carefully started to cut up the lavender, *was the only reason she was keeping him here.* Because it would be cruel, heartless, and inhuman to put Mr. Warwick back on the road when he could barely walk for more than ten minutes together. No other reason whatsoever.

"I'm sorry I can't call you a doctor, as you aren't one," came Mr. Warwick's voice.

Jenny was about to retort rudely, until she caught the genuine sadness in his tone.

Now that didn't make sense. How was it possible that he was truly sad at not being able to find it in himself to call her by her professional title?

"You have been very kind to me, Miss Powell," Mr. Warwick continued. "And I would like to appease you, if I could. But I cannot and will not give someone a title they have not earned."

Jenny snorted and turned, leaning on the table. "You think I haven't earned it?"

"How could you? You're a woman!" he pointed out, as though it were the most obvious reasoning in the world.

Taking a deep breath, Jenny tried to remind herself she knew this would be her lot.

The world, it appeared, was not ready for a female doctor. Or at least, England wasn't.

Mr. Warwick was examining her almost pityingly. "It's not your fault. It's just a fact of life."

And that was what did it. Not the words, though they were vexing. And not the tone, which was intended to be kind, Jenny was sure.

No, it was the way he looked at her. Those sympathetic eyes, that serious brow. The lilt of a smile which told her in no uncertain terms that Mr. Warwick, despite the fact she had saved his life . . . was sorry for her.

Well, she wasn't going to hold with that. Time for a little medicine he may not enjoy.

"I swear by Apollo the Physician, by Asclepius, by Hygieia, and Panacea, and by all the gods and goddesses, that to the best of my power and judgment I will faithfully observe this oath and obligation," said Jenny sternly.

Mr. Warwick's eyes bulged. "How on earth do you know that?"

"What, this? That the master who has instructed me in the art I will esteem as my parent? And supply them, as occasion may require, with the necessities of life?" asked Jenny innocently.

Goodness, it was pleasing to see the shock in the man's eyes. *He hadn't expected that, had he?*

"B-But . . . but . . . that's the Physician's Oath!" spluttered Mr. Warwick. "At least, I think it is. It's been a while since I sat in on a lecture on medicine, but—"

"His children I will regard as my own brothers. And if they desire to learn, I will instruct then in the same art without obligation or reward," Jenny said, continuing to recite. How long had it been since she had said this aloud? Too long, and yet every word was seared onto her heart.

Mr. Warwick was scowling now. "Fine, fine. You've made your point."

"I hope so," said Jenny, voice clear and eyes bright. "I don't like being disrespected in my own home, Mr. Warwick. Now you might not like the idea that it was I who saved you, but I did, though goodness knows why at the moment, given the thanks I've got!"

Her words rang out in the workroom, and guilt immediately seeped into her.

Jenny swallowed, dropping her gaze from Mr. Warwick to the wooden spoon.

What sort of a doctor was she? Demanding thanks? Throwing a petulant fit because she didn't feel as though she was being treated as impressively as she would want?

That wasn't why she had wished to study medicine. And if she waited around for sufficient thanks after all her hard work with each patient, she'd be standing at this table until the cows came home.

"What certifications do you have?" he demanded, and she looked up to see the proud jut of his chin.

Jenny rolled her eyes. Not this again. "Technically none, but—"

"Aha!" Mr. Warwick said triumphantly.

Irritation was bubbling up again, but she wasn't going to allow it to overcome her. She was a professional.

"Have you ever asked to see the certification of a doctor before?" she asked sweetly.

Mr. Warwick opened his mouth. Then closed it. "Uhmmm . . ."

Jenny waited. She managed to prevent herself from tapping her foot, but it took a great deal of effort.

"I . . . well," said Mr. Warwick awkwardly. "I didn't think—"

"That much is obvious," said Jenny with a rueful sigh as she went back to her work. "But then I don't know if I've been thinking much either."

She glanced at the carriage clock she kept on one corner of the table. Past one o'clock. Perhaps that was why their tempers were so raw.

"Hungry?" she said without looking round.

"Starving," came Mr. Warwick's voice behind her.

A smile crept across Jenny's face, despite herself. *Well, that was a good sign.* A man with an appetite was a man on the mend. Who was it that said that? It was in one of her books somewhere, though goodness knew which one.

"Let me get us both some luncheon," said Jenny, placing the wooden spoon on the table and giving up on the salve, for now.

"But your salve."

Her stomach jolted as she moved around the table to the little store in the darkest, coolest part of the room. Mr. Warwick had sounded there, just for a moment, as though he was truly concerned.

A trick of her ears, it must be. The man surely had no interest in her or her medicines.

"The salve will have to be done later," Jenny said heavily, pulling the pie dish to her.

Yes, there was enough there for two slices. If she could find some autumn lettuce, some carrots, perhaps even some—

"But you've been working hard since the crack of dawn," came Mr. Warwick's voice.

It almost sounded like concern.

No. Jenny was not going to convince herself, no matter how pleasant it would be, that Mr. Warwick was concerned about her. He was merely pointing out a fact. A fact anyone could have noticed.

At least, they would if there were anyone else around to witness it.

"And I shall be up just as early tomorrow, I'll be bound," said Jenny, straightening up and placing the pie dish on the table. "Let me find two plates . . ."

Her patient was thankfully silent as she put together a small luncheon. It wasn't much. A slice of chicken pie which was cold, though that was hardly unpleasant in the heat of the mid-September sun. A slice of ham. A handful of lettuce, picked that morning. And a carrot.

Jenny looked at the plates, tilting her head slightly as she tried to imagine what this Mr. Warwick would say about it. What did gentlemen have for luncheon these days?

She'd been giving him broth and gruel mostly, and porridge yesterday. Good, hearty stuff. But if he was itching to wander about the place, she would have to start feeding him something more substantial. And there was nothing more substantial than her chicken pie.

"Here," she said quietly.

Half dropping, half placing the plate on Mr. Warwick's lap, Jenny took hers to the other armchair and sat in it, eager to eat. How long had it been since breakfast?

"What is it?" Mr. Warwick said uneasily.

Jenny bit back her remark that it was food, and it was for him, and that should be good enough.

Just how wealthy was this gentleman? He had mentioned being able to pay the doctor once he returned home, and he had at no point inquired as to the cost of his care. Which suggested that it did not matter. That whatever the cost, he could meet it.

"It's chicken pie," Jenny said quietly, taking a bite of her own. When she swallowed, she added, "And poison."

Mr. Warwick's head jerked up. "And—"

"It's called a joke, Mr. Warwick," Jenny sighed. *Goodness, the man was hard work.* "You might want to try it sometime."

She met his gaze and thanked the stars above that the workroom was warm thanks to the afternoon sun. Her cheeks certainly weren't red because the handsome man had a way about him that made her suddenly very conscious of what she was doing with her hands.

"Thank you," Mr. Warwick said, somewhat begrudgingly.

Jenny did not answer. She watched the man lift the pie to his mouth, stomach twisting with anticipation. She was well rewarded for her silence by the sudden look of astonishment on Mr. Warwick's face.

He chewed, swallowed, then looked across in amazement. "But this—this is the best pie I have ever tasted!"

"I know," said Jenny with a laugh. "I mean, it usually is."

"But it's delicious!"

"I know," Jenny shrugged. "I know."

If there was one thing she could do almost as well as care for the sick and injured, it was cook. Her father hadn't liked it, forcing her out of the kitchen at least twice when she had been young, but Jenny had been unable to stay away. It was like magic, cooking. You put things together you would never think could even be together, then . . .

Then they created something fantastical.

Mr. Warwick took another eager bite and spoke with his mouth full, crumbs flying. "Where did you get it?"

Joy left her. "Get it? I baked it, of course."

With great difficulty, she wanted to say. *You try attempting to keep a fire the same steady temperature on one fireplace while you boil up a poultice on another.*

Mr. Warwick could not look any more relieved. "Oh, well. That makes sense."

Try as she might, Jenny could not help but feel smug. *Well, finally!* It was a relief to see he was finally going to start recognizing her talents. It had only taken—what, a week?

"Yes, that makes far more sense," he continued, the relief still visible on his face. "A woman's place after all, if she be not a lady, is in the kitchen."

Ice fell between them. Jenny stared. "I . . . I beg your pardon?" she said faintly.

"Yes, I'm glad to see you have been improving your feminine skills as you ought," Mr. Warwick said blithely, unaware he was digging his own grave with deeper and deeper strokes. "And a good cook will never struggle to find a husb—"

"If you continue that sentence the way I think you intend, I will scream, poison your next medicine, and bury your body in my garden where no one will find it," snapped Jenny.

Rage was curdling in her stomach, anger pumping through her veins. Her pulse was so thunderous she could hear her own pulse in her ears. Was that truly all this man thought a woman was good for? Serving him in whatever capacity most convenient to him at the time?

Mr. Warwick's mouth was agape. "You—you wouldn't—bury me in the garden?"

"Where no one will find it," Jenny snapped. She put her plate down with a clatter on the table beside her, luncheon only half eaten. "Now I don't want to hear a peep out of you for the next hour."

"But—"

"I have a salve to make!" she hissed, rising to her feet and advancing toward the wide-eyed gentleman. "I don't want to hear another word. Do you understand?"

Her chest was heaving, her lungs tight, and Jenny suddenly realized just how close she was to the miscreant. Only a few feet. It was far too close.

It was the rage that was doing it. The rage that was making her so warm.

Mr. Warwick nodded, eyes still large.

Jenny tried to slow her breathing. "Right. Good."

By the time she returned to the table, regret nudged her heart, but she pushed it away. *This Mr. Warwick! The sooner he was healthy and ready to leave, the better.*

CHAPTER FIVE

11 September 1811

MOSES GROANED. "IT'S so upsetting!"

"Expected, yes," said his unsympathetic companion. "That's what I was going to say."

Try as he might, Moses couldn't glare up at the woman. Though any expression he did send her way would have to be *up*. He didn't have much choice, lying as he was, on her workroom floor.

Oh, it was so humiliating.

"Did I, or did I not tell you that if you rushed about you would fall?" Miss Powell asked steadily.

Moses winced. There was something very specific about her tone that grated. It was the way a governess or a housekeeper spoke. The words themselves were not threatening, but the tone said without a shadow of a doubt that he had been bad.

Damnation. How did she do it?

"You did," he admitted, begrudgingly.

Trying to move his shoulder only brought pain, but he couldn't help but try it.

"Ouch!"

"Moses Warwick, you will be the death of yourself," Miss

Powell said with a sigh.

Moses tried to smile. "I thought the phrase was that I would be the death of you?"

"Oh, I wouldn't allow that to happen," she said lightly. "No, it would be you dying, not me."

He had to admit, she had a point.

Moses was going to have to accept—even if only in the privacy of his own mind—that he was not entirely healed. It was frustrating in the extreme, but there it was. Healthy men did not faint when they had been standing up for too long, for example.

Slowly, Moses lifted himself up and moved gratefully to the armchair that was fast becoming a sort of soft, comfortable prison.

He groaned. *Why did everything ache?*

"That's what you get when you fall onto a flagged stone floor," said Miss Powell, with absolutely no fellow feeling whatsoever. "Honestly, man. How many times have I told you to—"

"Yes, yes," Moses said testily. "I know."

He watched the woman's nostrils flare with a certain amount of satisfaction. Being trapped in a room with one person, even if she did retire upstairs to sleep, meant he had easily learned precisely what would most get under her skin.

Though it wasn't Miss Powell's skin he wanted to get under. It was that gown . . .

Moses cleared his throat. Not that he should be having such thoughts about the woman who had, arguably, rescued him. Why he had been returning to England in the first place, putting himself in a position to need rescuing, he still could not recall. That particular part of his memory had not returned—but it would. He was certain.

Whatever the reason, he would have died of exposure out there if Miss Powell had not brought him into her home. And for that, Moses supposed, he should be grateful.

"Now," Miss Powell said. "I—"

"Doctor?"

Moses's ears pricked up. *Surely there wasn't someone in this place calling this snippet of a woman doctor.*

It appeared there was—and more strangely still, Miss Powell seemed to expect it.

She certainly seemed to expect the visitor standing awkwardly on the threshold. "Ah, Mrs. Guernsey, there you are. Come on in. Ignore Mr. Warwick—I do."

Moses bristled, but then considered what Miss Powell would do if he were foolish enough to be disrespectful before another and pressed his lips firmly together.

As soon as he could walk for a significant amount of time, he would head to the nearest town. There would be a magistrate there, a lawyer, something. Someone who could take a message to Mr. Snee in London without it being intercepted. Anything he sent from here—well, East Langdon wasn't much to look at through the windows from his armchair. Goodness only knew what they'd do with a letter. Eat it, probably.

But until then, he would have to remain here. *And remain civil*, Moses reminded himself. He was the Duke of Chetnole. Surely he could stretch to civility.

He could not help but be curious, however, at the older woman who had come to "Doctor Powell." She looked respectable enough, in a day gown of yesteryear's fashion and a bonnet that had seen better days. So what on earth was she doing here?

"It's my sleep again, Doctor," she was saying to Miss Powell, who was listening seriously. "Oh, I lie there and I lie there, and sleep doesn't come! And the sun rises and I've had not a wink!"

The woman did sound exhausted. Try as he might, Moses could not stop listening to the conversation at the other end of the workroom.

This was his first time seeing Miss Powell truly in action. Other than caring for him, that was, and anyone could dump a man into a bed and wait for him to get better.

"I know how to stop a wound from bleeding and how to keep it

clean. Me. I'm the doctor. I'm the one who cared for you, and I'm the one who is losing patience."

Unconsciously, Moses reached to his shoulder where the wound was. Where the wound had been. The scab was still there, clearly with no sign of infection. He was going to be fine, as Miss Powell had pointed out curtly just the day before.

Had she done something? Kept the wound clean, as she had promised? Was there some sort of herbal remedy for that?

"I can quite understand your frustration, Mrs. Guernsey," Miss Powell was saying in a calm, considerate voice. "Come, sit at the table and I will fetch a remedy for you."

Moses did his best not to snort.

Remedy, indeed! It was a doctor this woman needed, or a different bed. He couldn't imagine what sort of thing they suffered for a mattress in a place like this, but if she'd ever slept on something like his bed at Chetnole Lacey . . . well, she wouldn't be complaining of a difficulty getting to sleep. A difficulty getting out of bed, now, that was more like it.

The clink of glass jars and bottles. He glanced over and was rewarded by the sight of Miss Powell bending over as she reached into her cabinet.

A smile trickled across Moses's face. *And what an excellent sight it was. By God, those buttocks could be a healing tonic all of themselves. If only he was back to full strength, then he could—*

"Tell me, Mrs. Guernsey," said Miss Powell, straightening up and glancing at Moses.

He quickly looked at his hands. When he chanced a look up again, Miss Powell was ignoring him and instead talking to her patient.

Her friend, Moses silently corrected himself. *Doctors have patients. Women have friends. Acquaintances. Enemies, he supposed.*

Not patients.

"—before you go to sleep?"

"Oh, I suppose what most people do before they go to bed," said Mrs. Guernsey blithely.

Moses could not help it. He snorted.

Mrs. Guernsey's cheeks flushed scarlet. "I-I meant—"

"I know precisely what you meant, Mrs. Guernsey," Miss Powell said evenly. "Completely ignore the brute in the corner there. I have attempted to teach him some manners, but apparently the thickest skulls can sometimes be too much even for me."

Moses scowled. *Well, what did they expect from him?* That was a hilarious jest—one that would have gone down heartily well at the Dulverton Club. Why shouldn't he laugh?

"Knitting is what you meant, isn't it, Mrs. Guernsey?" Miss Powell said kindly.

"Y-Yes, of course," stammered Mrs. Guernsey.

Miss Powell shot a defiant look over at Moses, who scowled, before turning back to her patient. *Friend. Damn it.*

"Now, when you knit . . ."

It was kind of her to spend so much time with the old woman. She didn't have to do this. Wherever Miss Powell got her money from, and it certainly wasn't from the people who visited occasionally to be given a poultice, or a plaster, or some sort of salve, it kept her in a relative life of luxury. For a woman.

If she had been a lady, born the daughter of a gentleman—that would be different.

"Tell me all about it," Miss Powell said with a gentle smile.

Mrs. Guernsey appeared to gain some boldness. "Well . . ."

He had to admit, though he would not do so aloud, that Miss Powell was good with people.

Not with him, though. Moses had never been treated so damnably ill, though he supposed if she knew she was actually caring for the Duke of Chetnole, she may do it with a little more consideration.

But the few people he had seen come to West Cottage to collect medicines and poultices had each been treated with decorum, tact, and kindness. Miss Powell truly listened to what they said, whatever the subject, even if it was drivel. She responded sometimes with far kinder words than he, Moses, would have bothered with.

Most unaccountable.

"And you do this by the fire?"

"By the fire in winter, and in the summer by a window. Though I will admit, there's been a chill in my bones recently, so I have lit a fire the last few nights."

What was even more unaccountable, Moses thought as he shifted uncomfortably in the armchair, *was how impressed he was.*

Impressed? With a woman?

It was not that women were inferior—far from it. In most cases, Moses had been rather disgruntled to discover that women were far superior than the men around them. Which only made it that much more frustrating that they didn't give their men a chance to improve themselves.

But Miss Powell was beyond anything he could have imagined. Bold when other women would have been reticent. Patient where most would have grown tired. There was something about her. A gentility of spirit, if not of temper.

And the trouble was, she was becoming fascinating.

Moses watched, enthralled, as Miss Powell gave the old woman absolute nonsensical advice which was surely done merely to placate her.

"—put the knitting down at least an hour before bed. Rinse your face, and your eyes, and ensure you only have one candle. And take this as you get into bed. It'll help," said Miss Powell confidently as she pressed the little blue bottle into the older woman's hands.

Even from this distance, Moses could see the tears sparkling in Mrs. Guernsey's eyes. "Oh, thank you, Doctor! Thank you!"

"Come back in a week if you have seen no improvement," said Miss Powell, gently leading the woman to the door. "Remember, just a small spoonful before bed. And no knitting!"

The door shut behind the grateful woman.

Then, and only then, did Moses permit himself to snort.

"Well, really!"

As he had known she would, Miss Powell turned on him in an instant. "What?"

Why did he do it? Was there something about her that made him wish to tease her? There was always a rather marvelous effect whenever he did so. She almost made it too easy.

Too enjoyable.

"Well," said Moses expansively, "telling her all that nonsense."

"Nonsense?" Miss Powell repeated, stepping around a table that was holding something fermenting in a jar and perching on a seat, elbows on the worn wood. "What on earth do you mean, nonsense? I just gave some rather important medical advice."

Moses snorted again and rolled his eyes for good measure. *This woman!* She needed to be taken down a peg or two. She surely couldn't think that telling an old woman not to knit in the evenings and to wash her face before bed was medical advice?

"I don't know how you can call yourself a doctor," he said quietly, shaking his head. "You demean the profession!"

"And you demean your entire sex, but I'm not here criticizing you about it," Miss Powell shot back with impressive speed.

Moses's pulse skipped a beat. *No, he was supposed to be angry. Not excited!*

"I don't know what you mean," he said coldly.

"Well, let me educate you then," said Miss Powell sweetly. "You may think you heard just a few strange little recommendations, and you may consider it nonsense."

"I do!"

"And you are perfectly welcome to your incorrect opinion," Miss Powell said, making Moses's temple throb.

"How can you say that?" he said desperately. "Fine, I admit, being able to recite the Physician's Oath—that was impressive. But it's probably written in one of your books over there! Anyone who can read could memorize it!"

It was a point well made. At least, Moses thought so. But for some reason, Miss Powell still looked unperturbed, as though she was completely secure in her knowledge.

It was . . . intoxicating.

It was irksome, Moses corrected mentally. *And not at all attractive.*

"Mrs. Guernsey knits every evening," Miss Powell said quietly, folding her hands in her lap. "Every woman in the village does. It's where they get most of their winter clothes from, and it brings in money if they can sell their work to any peddlers who come by."

Moses swallowed uncomfortably. *Talking about money! In broad daylight—to him, a gentleman! A duke!* Not that she knew that.

"And Mrs. Guernsey is a mature woman of wise years, and feels the cold, even now," Miss Powell continued. "She lights a fire and sits by it. Leaning close. Far too close."

Moses frowned. "And your point is?"

There was absolutely no need for Miss Powell to raise her eyes to the heavens, but she did so anyway. "Lord above, think, man! If you sit too close to a fire, what happens?"

Ah. He hadn't expected this to be turned back to him. "You . . . I don't know, get too hot?"

"And you get soot in your eyes," Miss Powell said, all patience gone. "Goodness, and you think I can't be a doctor! Mrs. Guernsey is spending hours, these light evenings, knitting over a fire that soots something terrible. By the time she goes to bed, her eyes are itching and sore. They keep her up, making it impossible to go to sleep! That's why it has come on so recently, with the cold snap!"

Moses's mouth fell open. It couldn't be that simple, could it? "And that . . . that's why she doesn't struggle to sleep in the summer. Because she knits—"

"By the window," Miss Powell completed triumphantly. She looked delighted. "Not knitting in the evening and washing her face, particularly her eyes, will make a great deal of difference. As will the jar I've given her. Now do you think what I said was nonsense?"

Well, no.

Moses could see it all now. It really was very simple. He was certain, if he'd been given more than half a second, he could have worked all that out himself. *Could he?*

It wasn't nice to feel a fool—but then, he had rather walked into it. There did not seem to be anything to do but debase himself before this woman.

Oh, how he hated doing this.

"I am sorry for having doubted you," he said stiffly. "I . . . well, I admit, I feel a tad foolish. You were clever, to work that out."

For a moment, Miss Powell just stared in astonishment.

Oh, come on! Him apologizing surely wasn't that unexpected!

"Well . . . that's progress, I suppose," she said dryly.

Her eyes met his, and a jolt of something most uncomfortable and yet highly delightful shot through Moses's chest.

It was as though the whole world had stopped. The sunlight streaming through the windows slowed, his pulse slackened, his very breathing seemed to pause.

Miss Powell was looking at him.

And not with ire. Not with frustration, which was generally the predominant expression on her face when she was looking at him.

No, this was different. This was interesting and intriguing and delightful. It made him want to stand and get closer to her. Take her hand, feel the sensation of her skin against his. Lean down and capture—

"You must find it lonely here," Moses found himself saying quietly.

Miss Powell shook her head as though she had been momentarily dazed. Was it possible—had she felt even a small smattering of what he had? "I like being alone," she said finally.

Moses grinned. "That's not the same thing, and you know it."

Well, would you look at that? It appeared they could have a rational conversation.

Miss Powell still looked dazed, and she hesitated before replying. "I . . . I have always found . . ." She licked her lips, and Moses most definitely did not look at the trail of shiny wetness now coating her bottom lip. Not at all. "It's always easier if I'm just on my own."

"On your own?"

Moses could not think of anything worse. Complete solitude was a punishment for him, though it wasn't as though he was enjoying anything much better here. Being cooped up in this workroom of hers, with only one woman—a woman who did not allow him to continuously talk or wander about the place?

It was worse than prison. It was torture.

"There's no one to please, no one to order me about," Miss Powell was saying with a dry laugh. "No one inspecting me or judging me. Telling me I should have done something one way or another. I just . . . do what I want."

Her look was defiant, and Moses could see she was twisting her hands in her lap.

She certainly preferred the quiet. He had never met anyone who was better entertained by her own mind for such lengths of time.

But this couldn't be it for her, could it? Miss Powell was surely engaged to be married or being courted by someone. She couldn't just be living out her life here in this cottage, in a small Kentish village that no one had ever heard of?

"But you're still alone," Moses pressed.

Miss Powell smiled, and for the first time, it was a natural one. Moses's stomach lurched. She truly was very beautiful. When she wasn't shouting.

"If that is the price I have to pay," she said lightly. "Besides, I've got the village."

"They only seem to come if they want something," Moses pointed out.

Perhaps it was not kind to say so, but he could not help it. He was right.

Miss Powell shrugged. "I suppose so."

"And they all accept you? As their 'Doctor Powell,' I mean?"

It was a question too far. Moses watched the shadow rush across her face. He saw the pain, the instinct to deny it, to suppress it. Pushing it far down within her. He saw just a hint of the loneliness, of the desperation for respect and for company.

"Some do," Miss Powell said lightly. "But not all. And that's far too much entertainment for you—be quiet while I measure out these herbs."

For once, Moses obeyed immediately. Whether or not she was surprised by his acquiescence, he was not sure. Miss Powell was leaning over the table, resolutely with her back to him.

What had to happen to a woman for her to end up here, all alone?

CHAPTER SIX

13 September 1811

T HE HUMORS, ONCE *considered to be unbalanced in those who displayed sickness, have long been understood to be only a partial comprehension of the body's complexity. Indeed, one when investigates further, the true scientist frequently discovers that the imbalance is far deeper than any cursory understanding of humors could possibly predict. The nature, therefore, of the investigative diagnosis must be taken with—*

"Miss Powell?"

Jenny did not look up. Could the man not see that she was busy? What did someone have to do in their own workroom to be left alone for more than five minutes?

"Later, Mr. Warwick," she said without looking away from her book.

Now, where was she?

The humors, once considered to be unbalanced in those who displayed sickness—

No, she'd read that bit.

Ah, here, right at the end of the page.

The nature, therefore, of the investigative diagnosis must be taken with great care. The patient will often be in a state of agitation—

"Miss Powell, what are you doing?"

Jenny sighed, allowing her shoulders to demonstrate the irritation she felt. "Reading a book, Mr. Warwick. Go back to sleep. I've told you, you must have one nap every after—"

"But I'm not tired," said Mr. Warwick with a snicker. Before she could stop him, the disobliging man had actually stepped out of the bed she had so graciously made up for him—*in her own workroom!*—and was walking toward her. "What are you reading?"

Jenny took a deep breath and tried to remember the "great care" the book she was reading recommended when dealing with patients. The trouble was, Mr. Warwick was enough to push any doctor, including the learned man who had written the large tome under her fingers.

It had been a long few days. Her in-house patient, Mr. Warwick, had initially grown in energy and had been almost bouncing round her workroom, getting in her way, preventing her from concentrating on her studies, causing a stir with her patients.

Irritation tingled at the edges of Jenny's chest. *Making her life difficult.*

Despite the clement weather, the man refused to take a stroll outside. Just around the cottage, Jenny had almost begged. Just spend more than a single minute outside her workroom . . .

Yet for some reason, he simply would not go out. If Jenny had not been convinced of the man's general disinterest in the world, she would have said he was . . . well, frightened.

Of what, she could not possibly say.

And then, as she had expected, the relapse. The man would refuse fresh air and gentle exercise? Well, it was no wonder he faded.

Yesterday, Mr. Warwick had spent almost the entire day in bed. Not feverish—Jenny had made sure of that. But he was not well. The wound on his shoulder looked a little pink. Her favorite poultice on his shoulder, a truly disgusting concoction down his throat, and stern orders to have an afternoon nap every day for a week were the remedy.

Jenny sighed. Not that Mr. Warwick appeared likely to listen to her. She should have given him the cod liver oil. That would have told him.

"What am I reading?" she repeated as the irritating man perched on one of the chairs at her large table.

Mr. Warwick grinned, a curl of hair falling over his eyes before it was brushed back. "It's a simple question, I would have thought."

Jenny glared. It was not, as he well knew, a simple question.

He had been too weak the last couple of days to argue with, so she had been forced to contend with him silently in her own head. That had been a mistake. The more Jenny thought about how Mr. Warwick refused to believe she could be intelligent enough to be a doctor, the angrier she became.

The cheek! When he is in her very workroom, day in and day out, seeing all the people that she cared for! When he himself was a recipient of her medical ministrations!

The only reason his shoulder wasn't oozing green and starting to twitch was because of her!

No, she needed to take the question as it was, at complete face value. The idiot wouldn't learn anything if she didn't teach him.

Besides, he was handsome.

She pushed the thought aside immediately. *He was not—*

Well. He was. But that was beside the point. The point was that she was not going to permit herself to be talked down to by a man who wouldn't even take simple instructions from someone who clearly knew what they were talking about!

"It's *A Modern Examination of the Human Body and Its Many Complexities*, by Doctor Barnabas Crackenthorpe," Jenny said shortly.

Dragging her eyes away from the intriguing—*irritating, irritating!*—man, she tried to concentrate. She had promised herself she would finish this chapter by the end of the week, and it was already Friday and she hadn't even finished the first page.

Where was she?

The nature, therefore, of the investigative diagnosis must be taken with great care. The patient will often be in a state of agitation, and in some cases, be entirely unreasonable—

"That's a bit steep for you, isn't it?" Mr. Warwick said, a teasing air in his voice.

Jenny's fingers tightened around the book. *Of all the ungrateful, infuriating, rude—*

When she looked up to give him a piece of her mind, he was grinning. "Never fear, I don't actually think that. I just wanted your attention, that was all."

Jenny's mouth fell open.

He . . . he was only saying that to annoy her? To get her to turn away from the page and instead look at him?

"You are a very self-centered man, you know," Jenny said conversationally, snapping the book shut.

Well, it wasn't as though she could get a single sentence read and actually understood with this man-child hanging about the place! She really should have been rid of him by now. She had told him—several times—that she would have a letter sent to anyone he wished so they could retrieve him.

In truth, she had said it with more and more vigor the last few days.

Didn't someone wish to know that he was safe? Jenny could not understand it—a man, any man, should have family, friends, servants, business partners. Someone!

But Mr. Warwick had merely laughed, said something about no one being worried about him, not yet, and declined her very kind offer.

"Self-centered? Yes, I suppose I am," said Mr. Warwick easily, leaning back in his chair. "It comes with the territory, I suppose."

"The territory—what, of being an invalid?" snapped Jenny.

He was enough to test anyone's patience, and hers had been sorely worn through these last few days.

Her workroom was supposed to be a place of calm, solace,

and most importantly, solitude. Yes, people came by from time to time—but for a visit. They came for a few minutes, thirty at the most, then they were gone.

Jenny had always prided herself on her ability to put aside her frustrations with the world, and her desire to be alone, and put up with people for that long. But Mr. Warwick had been here for days. Weeks. Really, she deserved a medal!

Never a moment to herself, never a chance to center herself. No silence, no ability to sit quietly and—

"You want to be reading again, don't you?" Mr. Warwick said conversationally.

A prickle of ire shot through Jenny. "Yes. Why don't you go away and—"

"You know, most people would be desperate to talk to me," he cut across her with a wide grin.

Jenny did everything she could to ignore the tingle that crept down her spine when he looked at her like that.

He's probably looked at countless women like that, she told herself sternly. *It didn't mean anything. In truth, it probably meant less. You know what men like that are like!*

Well. Not exactly. But she'd read about them. In books.

"And why on earth would anyone wish to talk to you?" Jenny asked, frustration escaping into her voice. "You're just a man, Mr. Warwick, and though I hesitate to inform you of this, your conversation leaves much to be desired!"

It was perhaps the most directly rude thing she had ever said to him. Maybe even the rudest thing she had ever said at all.

Yet for some reason, Mr. Warwick was grinning. *Grinning!*

"You know, you're the first person to ever say that to me—though I admit, I am sure people have whispered it behind my back," he said easily, as though the disparaging opinions of others meant little to him. "No one ever dares say it to my face."

Jenny laughed dryly. "And why is that?"

"Because I am Moses Warwick—"

"And that should impress me because?"

"—Duke of Chetnole," Mr. Warwick continued with a wry smile. "Goodness, Miss Powell, you do have a temper on you."

All she could do was stare. Stare, and think about the words Mr. Warwick had just said as they rang through her mind.

Duke of Chetnole. Duke of Chetnole?

No. Jenny was certain there could not be a duke in her workroom. She would have known—there would have been something about him that would have immediately testified to his higher nobility. A sense of his respectability, perhaps.

Something!

But as her mind whirled, it reminded her that the man she had known as Mr. Warwick had been found without papers, luggage, or transport. Clearly stabbed in the back, undoubtedly robbed, left for dead just a few yards from her cottage.

There had been nothing of him, save for the clothes on his back, and they had been in a shoddy state of repair, even if they had once been fine.

Did dukes wear shirts with holes in them? Were dukes often attired in waistcoats with missing buttons?

"You—you are a duke?" Jenny murmured, her chest tight.

It couldn't be.

Mr. Warwick—if that was his name—grinned. He did so with refined elegance, as though he were turning on a switch and suddenly transforming himself. The awkwardness was gone, the casual manner with which he sat was gone. Suddenly his back was straight, his manners more stylish. There was a greater sense of power about him. Comfortable in anyone's company—no, more than that. More like anyone around him was fortunate indeed to even be in his presence.

"I am a duke," he said with a grin. "Surprise, I suppose."

Jenny swallowed.

Well, there was no mistaking it now. She had seen a duke once, from afar. The Duke of Martock had been very gracious in talking to almost everyone in the room, but she had not sought a moment with him. Seeking a moment with anyone was something Jenny did not typically do. She liked her privacy, her silence. She had wished to return home.

But there had been something about that duke, and it was the same with this man. A sense, coming from within them, that the world owed them something.

Jenny let out a heavy sigh. "Dear God. Well, you've made a right fool of me."

She had spoken quietly, but a dull, resigned sense had somehow seeped into it as her shoulders slumped.

Living this down was not something she would ever achieve. The way she had spoken to him! She had ordered him about, shouted at him, forced him to drink some of her concoctions which could, she would now admit, have included a touch of honey to take the bitterness off.

Her name would be mud—at least, the few people who still knew of her would now consider her name to be mud. And her mother—

"Fool?" said Mr. Warwick in surprise.

No, that wasn't right, was it? He wasn't Mr. Warwick—he was the Duke of Chetnole.

Jenny cringed. And she had thought his name ridiculous, thought it was a false name! Who, after all, was named Warwick?

Dukes, apparently.

"No, it's not like that," the duke was saying. "I kept my true name a secret merely because I needed to ascertain you weren't—"

"Weren't what?" said Jenny, rising hotly and stepping forward with restless energy.

The nerve of the man! First he lied, then he took advantage of her medical knowledge while denying she even had any, insinuated she might have an ulterior motive in speaking with him, and then, worst of all . . . he wouldn't let her read her book!

"Well, the sort of person to take advantage," said the duke softly, still seated.

Jenny frowned, shifting from foot to foot. "Take . . . take advantage?"

She blushed even as she repeated the words. It was the sort of thing her mother would have said.

"I merely meant that you could have exacted from me a hefty price for saving my life," the duke was saying. "There are some who would have even attempted to orchestrate . . . well, a loss of honor, if you catch my drift."

Jenny stared as the man grinned, a mischievous look in his eye. *What on earth was he driving at?*

"I don't," she said stiffly.

The duke waved a graceful hand. "Oh, we've been left alone together too long, with my bed in here, highly irregular, the only thing to save my honor is to marry—"

"Yes, yes, I get the idea," said Jenny hastily, cheeks burning as she glanced over at the pallet on the other side of her workroom.

Yes. Well, she certainly would not have done such a thing if she had known.

Or would she? Where else could she have put him? It was not as though she would have been able to drag him upstairs—it had been hard enough getting the man the twenty yards into her cottage in the first place.

"And you didn't ask questions of 'Mr. Warwick.'"

Jenny's attention returned to him in a flash. "And should I have?"

But he was right. She would have considered it the height of rudeness to make demands of her patients, beyond that which could help her cure them. And now that the Duke of Chetnole had pointed it out, Jenny could see that, had she known his true identity, she would have had a great many questions.

What was a duke doing out here all alone? Where were his carriage, his servants? Should they not have been able to fight off an attack of the magnitude he had suffered? Where had he been going? This road led only to the sea.

Ah, of course. To the sea.

Jenny shook her head. "Well, I did not have you down as someone serving your country, Your Grace. I rather had you pegged as someone who only served your own interests."

It was a low blow, but she was riled and confused and hurt. He had lied to her—a lie of omission, to be sure, but a lie nonetheless. He had taken advantage of her.

Oh, not in that way. That wasn't the sort of thing that happened to her. But still.

The Duke of Chetnole had risen slowly. "Serve my own interests?"

Jenny swallowed. He was so much taller than her. He had spent so much time in her workroom lying down that she always forgot. "Well, haven't you been doing that while you've been here?"

"I'm only here because I was stabbed in the back in France," said the duke quietly, the timbre of his low voice thrumming in Jenny's chest most unaccountably. "Being a spy for one's country, it can lead to difficulties."

How did he do it? Though still a few feet from her, Jenny was overcome with a sense that the duke was close. Very close. Whispering in her ear.

It was most unsettling. That, surely, was the only reasonable explanation for the swooping of her stomach, the way she felt warm and cold all over, both at the same time.

"And you know dukes—and spies—can do whatever they want," the duke continued, taking a step toward her.

Jenny took a step back.

At least, that was what she should have done. It was the instinct she had, yet her legs did not obey. Not while her eyes were gazing up into the light blue fire dancing in the Duke of Chetnole's eyes.

How had she never noticed, when tending to his shoulder, just how broad he was? How tall, how majest—

Jenny gasped as the Duke of Chetnole's mouth closed on hers.

His kiss was like him: determined, fierce. Taking what he wanted, little thought for her.

At least, that was how it started. Jenny had lifted her hands to push him away, to demand he never do such an outrageous thing again, and perhaps even instruct him to send for a few servants and have them carry him away.

She really was going to do it.

But in that instant, as her hands pressed against the soft fabric of his shirt, something changed. The Duke of Chetnole gently parted her lips, reverentially and without demands, and the pleasure that soared through Jenny was unlike anything she had ever known.

She whimpered.

No one had ever touched her like this. Had claimed possession of her mouth like this. Had teased tendrils of delight through her body with just one kiss, one connection, one heady—

He pulled away.

Jenny blinked, dazed in the brilliant brightness of his presence. *She shouldn't have enjoyed that.*

"Damn," muttered the Duke of Chetnole.

There was a rather dazed expression on his face, as well—almost as though . . .

Jenny's stomach twisted uncomfortably. Almost as though he had enjoyed it too.

Oh, why did she want him to enjoy it? Why did she crave his approval, to know he had been transported just as swiftly as she had?

"I—that is not the sort of medicine I would typically prescribe," Jenny said sternly.

At least, she had intended for her words to be stern. Unfortunately, there did not appear to be sufficient breath in her lungs for her words to have much weight.

The irritating Duke of Chetnole seemed to spot that. He grinned. "I should damn well think not! God, Miss Powell, you'd have every man in the county here—"

The slap was strong, echoed around the workroom, and hurt Jenny's hand.

Dear God, how did anyone fight if just a simple slap was going to smart so?

Wringing her hand, Jenny leveled a stare as best she could at the man she had just attacked. *Imperious, that's what she needed to look like.* "Never, ever, say something like that to me again."

The Duke of Chetnole was staring, his cheek red. No, both his cheeks. Was it possible—could it be that he was in some way ashamed of what he had said?

"I apologize," he said stiffly. "I should not have—"

"No, you should not," Jenny said, mouth dry. "And you never will again."

Should not have said that. Should not have kissed her. Should not have entered her life without any thought for the consequences, making it difficult to concentrate on her books. Difficult to spend all day without any respite. Difficult to stop thinking about him . . .

"I . . . I think I'll go for that nap now," the duke said quietly.

Jenny did not trust her voice. She nodded smartly, then stepped away from him toward the table. Her book, *A Modern Examination of the Human Body and Its Many Complexities*, was still waiting. How she would manage to take in a single word after that altercation, however . . . she did not know.

CHAPTER SEVEN

17 September 1811

"**I** AM ABSOLUTELY sure," said Moses uncertainly.

Well, this was damned strange. He had never been one for staying indoors, but when his shoulder had ached with every movement, what incentive had he for actually going outside?

And now . . .

He couldn't explain it. But it was as though by staying inside for so long as he had been recuperating with Miss Powell, he had somehow grown accustomed to being inside.

Going outside, in fact, seemed like a foolish idea. Dangerous.

It was complete idiocy, Moses thought as he pulled on a stuffy, slightly mothy jacket Miss Powell had procured for him. Going outside was not going to hurt him. There was no one out there who even knew him. They just thought him a particularly pathetic patient of Miss Powell's. Which he was.

Try as he might, he could not stop looking at the way the sunlight drifted through the window and transformed Miss Powell's chestnut hair to gold. Or the way she forced another pin into her stubborn curls, the pencil having been removed. Or how her collarbone—

"I said that you were ready to go out, and you are," said Miss

Powell determinedly, pulling on her pelisse with what appeared to be unnecessary force. "And it's high time you were out of here."

Moses winced.

Did she mean that? Was his presence in her home so irksome as all that? Was she merely desperate for him to leave?

"Fresh air," Miss Powell continued. "Something you've been lacking these last few days. A walk to the end of the village and back."

"And you'll be with me?"

Moses hated the uncertainty in his voice. He was a duke! The Duke of Chetnole! He was a spy, had spent months in France gathering information and eluding all French capture. He wasn't afraid of a walk to the end of a village! And yet . . .

Moses swallowed. Whatever fear had entered his heart while he had remained ensconced in this cottage of hers, he had to purge it. He couldn't grow fearful of the world just because he had been absent from it.

"We need to see how your strength is bearing up," Miss Powell was saying as she wrapped a woolen scarf around his neck. "You'll be home—I mean, back before you know it."

Moses could not help it. He caught Miss Powell's eye.

Heat roared through him as her fingers tidied the scarf around his neck. Was she thinking about it, as well? The moment he had thrown all caution to the wind and kissed her? The instant he had felt something far deeper, far darker than he could ever have imagined?

Did she think about it often, as he did? Did it haunt her daydreams, intrude on her thoughts, seep into her dreams making it impossible to—

"There," said Miss Powell stiffly, stepping away toward the door. "Keep up."

Moses swallowed.

Of course she didn't, he thought. He could focus on the way he'd felt during that kiss all he liked, but he could not ignore how it ended.

"I should damn well think not! God, Miss Powell, you'd have every man in the county here—"

That had been when she'd slapped him. Hard.

"I apologize. I should not have—"

"No, you should not."

Miss Powell had made it perfectly clear what she felt toward Moses. Not much at all.

"Bracing fresh air!" came Miss Powell's voice ahead of him, the sight of her now gone as she stepped out of the workroom. "Keep up, Mr. Warwick!"

Moses could not help but smile. They had agreed that, while he was out in East Langdon, it was probably best no one else knew he had a title. Or a fortune. Or a country estate far larger than the village itself.

Best to keep that between them.

"Coming," he called out.

Glancing back at his makeshift bed and wishing he could disappear right back into it, Moses sighed and stepped through the door into the hall—a door he had not passed through since Miss Powell had dragged his unconscious body into the house.

He had not known, particularly, what to expect beyond the workroom. The structure itself did not seem to be lavish, but all he had seen was that one large room where Miss Powell seemed to spend almost all her time.

It was therefore with great surprise that Moses saw a painting on the wall of the hall he was now standing in that looked remarkably like a Gainsborough.

A Gainsborough? Here, in a country cottage of a woman pretending to be a doctor?

"Miss Powell," Moses called after the woman who had already reached the front door. "What—"

"No time for that," she said smartly, throwing open the door. "Come on!"

There appeared to be no point in arguing with her. Moses

had discovered that early in his time here, though admittedly he had spent the greater part of the first week unconscious, as far as he could tell. He only had Miss Powell's word for it that it was now the middle of September.

But when he stepped outside and took in the chilling air, he had to admit that this was not August, not anymore.

"Ah, Doctor Powell!"

Moses glared at the young man who approached and slammed the door behind him.

The man hesitated. "And . . . and friend."

"Patient," said Miss Powell smoothly as she stepped across the path to speak with the youth. "How are you, Mr. Jones?"

"Oh, as well as can be, Doctor," said the man gratefully, his attention still flickering over to Moses who remained by the front door. "I must say, that poultice you gave me, it has truly worked wonders . . ."

Moses snorted, though made sure to do so quietly.

Country folk! They were so easily impressed, so easily won over. Why, he was certain that whatever small ailment the young man had, a doctor in London would have cured in half the time.

Though, a voice at the back of his mind remarked, *probably for twice the expense.*

Moses pushed the thought away. The point was, a doctor like that would have learning. Expertise. He would be able to heal people!

Unlike your shoulder, then, nudged the irritating voice. *Nothing like that.*

Shifting on his feet and marveling at how loose his shoulder felt, Moses tried not to watch the way the young man smiled at Miss Powell.

Doctor Powell, indeed. Well, it was clear what the young man wanted, and that was Miss Powell. Calling her that ridiculous title was surely an excuse to get into her good books. *Not something he would ever do,* Moses thought righteously.

"Mr. Warwick?"

He had been honest with her—told her his opinion and not thought to conceal it just to make her smile. Not that he had made her smile, not often. It was strange, actually—

"Mr. Warwick!" snapped Miss Powell.

Moses blinked. "Wh-What?"

"I asked if you were ready to commence our walk, but you were obviously thinking of something far more pleasant."

His cheeks flared with heat. "I-I was?"

"You certainly looked like it," said Miss Powell. Mr. Jones appeared to have gone. "You were smiling."

An awkward moment fell between them, one Moses did not know how to end. What was it about this woman who always seemed to guess at what he was thinking, even when—especially when—it was about her?

"A walk," he said firmly.

"That's what I've been—never mind," sighed Miss Powell, turning from him and toward the path. "This way."

The village, as she called it, was not very large. Moses was hardly sure whether it could, in truth, be called a village.

Miss Powell's cottage was a little out of the way, but ten minutes of walking down the lane and a few more scattered houses appeared. Then there was a green, upon which faced a church, a pub, and some manner of store of all sorts. Then a few more houses. And that was it.

"This is it?" Moses foolishly said aloud.

Miss Powell frowned. "What, you were expecting Mayfair?"

He tried to grin. "Not quite."

Not quite, but he had expected more than this. How could she, someone like Miss Powell, happily live in a village as small as this? Was not her circle incredibly small? Surely her acquaintance of respectable people was tiny!

Though now he came to think about it, Moses could not recall Miss Powell receiving any guests. Visitors, certainly. She would call them patients. But no guests, no friends. She dined with him, simple fare, delicious fare. And then she would read, and then she would go to bed.

Moses glanced at Miss Powell as they walked sedately around the village green. *Surely this life could not satisfy?*

"Doctor Powell! Oh, how wonderful to see you in the village!" Mrs. Guernsey rushed over to them, eagerly reaching out to shake the young woman's hand. "You won't believe it, but that tonic you've given me, it's working wonders! I am sleeping through the night without a care in the world!"

Miss Powell smiled as her hand was tightly squeezed. "And your knitting?"

"Oh, I obeyed that instruction, too, never you fear!" prattled on Mrs. Guernsey. "But that tonic! I don't know what you put in it . . ."

Over the little old woman's head, Miss Powell looked up and met Moses's eye. She grinned.

Moses's stomach lurched. *By God, she was a clever one.* She had been right. The knitting by the fire had led to sore eyes, and that had led to a lack of sleep. Now the poor dear had stopped knitting, and all of a sudden she was better, even if she did think it was the tonic. Goodness, this village didn't deserve someone like Miss Powell.

"Oh, it's Doctor Powell!" came another voice.

Moses turned with surprise to see the vicar step out of the little house beside the church. Well, the man would wish to—

But instead of making straight for him, as was befitting his rank, the vicar bowed and beamed at Miss Powell. "Doctor Powell, I must thank you. That ointment you made up for me— my hands are so much better! I can even hold a pen again! Really, you do work wonders—"

"It's like I said about my sleeping!" interrupted Mrs. Guernsey, who seemingly wished to have a monopoly on the young woman. "Never known anything like it—"

"Sermons can once again be written!" said the vicar rapturously. "And it's all thanks to you, Doctor Powell—"

Moses snorted.

The three inhabitants of East Langdon all turned to him.

Oh, blast.

"Don't mind him," said Miss Powell serenely. "This is Mr. Warwick. An invalid who is staying with me while he recuperates from a great injury—a charity case."

Moses bristled. *A charity case? How dare—*

"Yes, no payment has exchanged hands and yet I still care for him," Miss Powell said with a teasing smile only Moses seemed to notice. "It is important, isn't it Reverend, that we help the less fortunate?"

"Oh, my goodness me, yes, yes," said the vicar distractedly, staring at Moses. "I had no idea . . ."

"I did," said Mrs. Guernsey importantly. "I saw him, didn't I—didn't I, Doctor Powell?"

"That you did," said Miss Powell smoothly. "And now if you will excuse us, I must ensure my patient continues his exercise. I must check his strength has returned."

There were a few more pleasantries exchanged, but Moses wasn't entirely sure what they were because his mind was humming with the injustice of it all.

Charity case indeed!

Well, yes, he hadn't exactly paid Miss Powell. But he'd been robbed, all money taken. And until his full memory returned, he could not send for help or even post a note to a friend saying where he was.

Why had he returned from France?

That was the question he had to answer.

"—next week, and it'll be ready for you," Miss Powell was saying. "Good day."

"Good day," chorused the vicar and Mrs. Guernsey, staring curiously at Moses as he fell into step beside Miss Powell.

Only when he was certain they had put sufficient distance between them and her happy customers did he snap, "Charity case?"

"I thought it rather an apt description, actually," said Miss

Powell with a dry laugh. "You have to admit, it is technically true."

Struggling with his frustration as they continued their way around the village green, Moses tried to swallow his ire.

This was outrageous! He had never been presumed to be *poor*, never in his life. Even when he had been a spy, he had clearly been a gentleman. The French may not have liked him, and most of them had not trusted him, but they had at the very least spoken to him with respect.

But Miss Powell—

"Good afternoon, Doctor."

"Good day, Doctor Powell."

"Doctor Powell, your health."

Moses cleared his throat. "Everyone seems to know you."

It was true. They could not step more than five feet along the path without someone inclining their head, bowing, or smiling at the young woman.

And they all called her the same thing: Doctor Powell.

Miss Powell was smiling sedately. "Everyone does, even if they do not trust me. But when a child has a fever, or a husband could lose work due to injury, trust does not usually come into it."

They were meandering out of the village and back onto the lane leading to her cottage.

Moses nodded sagely. "Desperation will do that to people."

"And they are desperate," said Miss Powell quietly.

He glanced at her. There did not appear to be any malice in her voice, nor frustration on her face. "And it doesn't bother you?"

She halted. They were away from any buildings and there was not a single other person on the path. They were alone.

Miss Powell raised a hand to pull back a branch from the hedgerow, inspecting it as though it were her crop and she were a farmer. "And why should it bother me?"

Moses stared. *Surely she could not be that ignorant.* "Well. That they disparage you and distrust you when they have no need of you, and when they do—"

"They come a-calling?" Miss Powell said lightly.

His stomach lurched.

"No, it does not bother me," she said quietly. "Perhaps once it did. Perhaps once I thought I was owed something by those I lived amongst. But I soon learned that whether I treated them or not, I still had to live with myself. It's my own self-respect that matters to me the most, Your Grace. Not theirs."

Moses swallowed.

Well, that was impressive. This woman, she never ceased to impress, even when she was saying something that surely could not be true. It would take a true saint to live amongst such contrary people, would it not?

"You judge them harshly."

"I do not think you judge them harshly enough," Moses said honestly, the words slipping from his tongue. "You do not wish to be admired, then?"

"Ah, that is a completely different matter, and one that I am far less sanguine about," said Miss Powell with a laugh. "You see, Your Grace—"

"Moses."

What had possessed him to say such a thing? But Moses could not take it back now—and he had no wish to, as he saw the flush on Miss Powell's cheeks.

Now that was interesting.

"I-I cannot call you that," Miss Powell said, stepping away from the hedgerow and toward him. "You must know, I cannot—"

"Not in public, certainly," said Moses with what he hoped was a smile. "But when it is just the two of us, as it so often is, I . . . well, I would like you to call me Moses."

I would like you to do many other things, he thought. *But those aren't things I can say. No gentleman would.*

"You would, would you?" Miss Powell said, arching an eyebrow.

Moses fought the instinct to pull her once more into his arms and kiss her soundly. Kiss her longer, deeper, harder than he had in her workroom. Show her what it was to be kissed by a man who was devoted to—

Devoted? Now where had that thought come from?

"Moses," Miss Powell repeated, her cheeks still pink. "Well, I suppose I can try it. Does that mean you should be permitted to call me Jenny?"

Something stirred, deep within. Well, perhaps more down than within. But certainly no further down than his knees.

He swallowed, mouth dry. "If . . . if you will consent to it."

Jenny—he could no longer think of her as Miss Powell, even if he should—examined him with a steady eye. Nothing could escape her notice. It was one of the things he most admired about her. Unfortunately for him, that list appeared to be ever growing.

"Fine," said Jenny briefly. Then she started walking slowly toward her cottage.

For a moment, Moses stood in the lane in complete shock. *Fine? So . . . so she had consented?*

"Jenny?" he tried.

The woman the entire village of East Langdon appeared to depend upon stopped and glanced over her shoulder. "Don't tell me you are too weak to walk back to my cottage."

Moses puffed out his chest. *Too weak!* "Just . . . just checking something."

He had reached her side within a moment and fought the temptation to take her hand and place it on his arm. He was a duke, yes, but this was not—this was not London. Nor Bath. This was a tiny Kentish village where no one, save Miss Powell—save Jenny, knew who he was. He did not have to act the duke all the time.

"You are kind," he said quietly. "To tend to so many of them."

Jenny gave a laugh. "I think even you would find it hard to turn away someone who arrived at your door inconsolable."

"Perhaps so," Moses conceded. "But what about the proper doctor?"

The instant the words had left his mouth, he realized his

mistake—but it was a mistake he could not take back.

"Proper doctor," Jenny repeated coldly. "What precisely is that supposed to mean?"

"I just—"

"I am a proper doctor, even if you do not personally like to own it," she said in an icy tone. "I attended every lecture, even performed—and I don't have to explain myself to you!"

Somehow there had appeared between them a gap of several feet. Moses could not understand it—had she not been standing right beside him?

Still, there was nothing for it. "I meant a man and you know—"

"A man?" Jenny repeated. Even her eyes were cold, which made no sense. Mere minutes ago there had been such warmth there. "Still pressing that idiotic point, Mr. Warwick?"

Mr. Warwick. Not Moses. Not even Your Grace.

His heart sank. "You must know you're out of step with the world, Jenny—"

"And that makes me wrong, does it?"

Irritation curled around his conscience, overpowering it. "Why do you have to make this so difficult?"

"Why do you?" Jenny shot back. They had almost reached her cottage now, but all the camaraderie had gone from the day. "Let's pretend just for a moment that you are right, which you are not. Who here in East Langdon could afford a *proper* doctor?"

Moses opened his mouth, hesitated, then closed it again.

Oh, damn and blast it, but he hadn't considered that.

Jenny had a look of sad triumph. "Not everyone is a duke, Your Grace. We don't have the luxury of picking and choosing the way we get to live. Some of us have to do what is before us. Some of us have only the choice ahead of us. Perhaps you should remember that, the next time we go for a walk to the village. After you."

Moses swallowed. She slammed open the front door, clearly waiting for him to enter.

He had to open his stupid mouth.

CHAPTER EIGHT

20 September 1811

"Y OU'RE DISTRACTING ME," Jenny found herself saying for the third time that morning.

Moses looked up. "I'm just sitting here!"

"You're tapping," she pointed out, trying to ignore the fact that if she had not been so focused on the man in the first place, she would not have noticed. "Tapping."

"I am?" said Moses innocently from the armchair.

Jenny tried to ensure her face was arranged in a nonchalant manner.

Because she wasn't completely absorbed by what the handsome gentleman was doing in her workroom. She wasn't constantly conscious of where he was. What he was doing. How he was breathing . . .

And she certainly wasn't thinking of the Duke of Chetnole as "Moses." Even though he had asked her to. Even though he'd called her Jenny, and made her heart sing, and—

"Don't tap," she said sternly, turning back to her book.

Strange. *A Modern Examination of the Human Body and Its Many Complexities* had always been something of a comfort read, but for the last few days, it simply had not given her the respite she wanted.

Worst of all, nothing now offered her that comfort. Whenever she tried to settle, do something, make up a lotion, review the stock of herbs, write out a list of the things she had to do before the winter . . .

There he was.

Moses. Doing something. Anything, in truth, was enough to distract her. After the stern words she had exchanged with him only a few days ago, their conversation had been rather stilted. After all, where do you go after that?

"Not everyone is a duke, Your Grace. We don't have the luxury of picking and choosing the way we get to live. Some of us have to do what is before us. Some of us have only the choice ahead of us. Perhaps you should remember that, the next time we go for a walk to the village."

Jenny's chest tightened, but she forced herself to stay calm.

It is because you have not had enough time to yourself, she thought silently. *You need time alone to recenter yourself, you always have, and now . . . now you don't have it. Now you're constantly in the company of a man who thinks it appropriate to—*

"Will you stop tapping!" Jenny said, looking up.

Moses appeared to be the picture of innocence. "I don't even know I'm doing it!"

"Stop it," she said sharply. "Think about it—how can you not know you're tapping?"

It boggled the mind. It beggared belief. And it was bothersome in a way Jenny could not explain.

"I am sorry," said Moses meekly.

Jenny frowned. Something bad was going to happen when that man was so . . . appealing.

Appeasing. That was what she had meant to think. Appeasing. Not appealing. Not appealing at all.

After all, who would find a gentleman, a nobleman, lounging about the place with his feet over the arm of his chair, lying back with his shirt unbuttoned at the top, a lazy grin on his—

Jenny forced herself to look back at the book.

"You know what I think?" came Moses's voice from behind her.

"What do you think?" Jenny said, turning to him, giving up what was quickly becoming a futile attempt to read.

But just for a moment. At any time she could look away and return to her book. It wasn't as though she were actually enjoying his presence or anything. No, any brief feeling of being drawn to him or possibly wanting to know what he was thinking now—that was just a touch of loneliness, she told herself. Even a woman who enjoyed solitude needed to speak to others once in a while. Was that not what she had told half the village, that the old and the infirm needed to be visited?

"I think you're growing accustomed to having me around," said Moses with a grin.

Jenny's mouth fell open. "You do?"

How could he think that? The value of occasional conversation notwithstanding, it was slow torture, never having the place to herself. Always having to explain what she was doing. Telling him the different ingredients she was using. Discussing the various schools of thought on lavender for sleep or calming. Arguing with him about the difference between a lotion and a poultice. Explaining—

Now she came to think of it, and Jenny's stomach squirmed at the thought, she *had* rather got accustomed to having him around.

"I think you'd hate the quiet if I were to go out for a solitary walk to the village," said Moses matter-of-factly.

Jenny rose without thinking and stepped across the workroom, past the fire where that evening's stew was bubbling, and sat in the armchair opposite Moses.

"I'm not sure whether I could convince you to leave," she said. "I think you've got far too accustomed to having someone wait on you hand and foot."

"Oh, it's not that different to being a duke, really."

She had to laugh at that. "But rather different from being a spy, I suppose."

A spy. It was something they hadn't discussed, despite her interest in the topic. Jenny supposed Moses would not be able to tell her much, even if he wanted to.

And it had changed him in her eyes, if only a smidgen.

He was most certainly a duke. There was a laziness in his expression at times, an assumption in his air that everything would be done for him, and at once. But there was also a sharpness. An intellect. The sense, somehow, that if required, he would work just as hard as or perhaps even harder than any other man to accomplish a goal.

Jenny swallowed. It was a most disconcerting feeling. One she liked, despite herself.

"Being a spy is certainly very different from being a duke," Moses was saying. "In fact, I think that is partly why I decided to join and serve my country. I know I had to come back for a reason, but I . . . I can't recall why."

She examined him closely. He did not seem to be lying.

"I wanted to be needed," Moses said quietly. "Not just an accessory, an impressive name on someone's guestlist. I wanted to be something more."

"I understand."

The gentleman raised an eyebrow.

"I do!" said Jenny with a wry laugh. "You may think I cannot possibly understand, but . . . you are going to have to trust me on this. I . . . I know what it is to be considered nothing more than an accessory."

Her mouth was dry, but she could not—would not—give him any information. He could not be trusted with it.

"Well, you aren't a duke," Moses said with a shrug. "Just expected the stand about or play bridge or such like. Bored out of my skull within three months of leaving university—that's why I suppose I'm a spy."

She frowned. "Simply because spying is not like being a duke? Who wouldn't want to be wealthy, important, able to order people about?"

Moses's eyes twinkled. "That's a fair representation of being a duke."

Jenny flushed. She had not intended to be rude. "I just meant—"

"I know what you meant—but I meant what I said. There's very little of interest in being a duke," he said quietly. "I am a person who bores easily. Who tires of having to sit about and listen to dull conversation about the changing fashion of sleeves, or whether one's horse won at Ascot. I'd rather be doing something. Serving."

She could not help but smile. "Perhaps we have something in common after all."

Jenny tried to ignore the swooping sensation in her stomach. The trouble was, that only made it more obvious that her pulse was beating a little faster.

"Miss Powell?" came an intruding voice from the hall.

Jenny rose so swiftly, she almost tripped over her own feet. "Yes?"

Oh, that someone had to come in and interrupt what had been a moment she had rather been enjoying!

Though perhaps just in time. The last thing she needed was for her emotions to get foolishly tangled up with a dangerous duke.

"There you are," said the voice. "And—ah. Your charity case."

Jenny stifled a laugh as she went to formally greet Mr. Saunders with a curtsey. "News travels fast."

"I'll have you know—"

"Mr. Warwick, I think it's time you rested that voice of yours," said Jenny over her shoulder, trying not to laugh at the look of outrage on Moses's face. "I have a patient."

She turned back to Mr. Saunders and tried to maintain the smile Moses had sparked.

Mr. Saunders. She had spoken the truth to Moses a few days

ago when she told him she did not mind serving the people of East Langdon even though they did not all respect her.

But Mr. Saunders was, perhaps, an exception.

Still. His rudeness did not need to mean she was rude in return.

"How can I help you, Mr. Saunders?"

"I do not think you can, Miss Powell, but I came because the wife said I had to," said the man shortly.

Jenny's smile faded, no matter what she attempted. But her careful eye had been flicking over the man. It did not take a genius to tell what the matter was. He was standing all wrong.

"Your knee again?"

Mr. Saunders flushed. "She's told you, then."

"No, it's the way you're standing," said Jenny, her voice fading as she stepped around the man, taking a close look. "The left, it's giving you pain. Plowing?"

"I can't walk eight mile behind a plow to furrow an acre, not with this leg," said Mr. Saunders, face red as he admitted the weakness. "I told her, the missus, I told her—"

"Walk forward for me," Jenny instructed.

The man did not move. *Why would he*, she thought wearily. It was always the ones sent by their wives who were the most difficult. Sometimes she wished they would not come at all.

Mr. Saunders was still glowering. "I walked all the way here. I don't want to—"

"And if I had seen you walk all the way here, I would have an idea of how to help you," said Jenny evenly. "Please, Mr. Saunders. Just a few steps."

His glower did not diminish, but the man did deign to step forward until he reached the table.

Then he turned with a dour expression. "So, I'll go home and tell the wife—"

"Tell her you need to put a poultice on your leg every evening when you get home," said Jenny confidently, stepping over to one of her cupboards. "Keep the foot elevated. And have a look at your plow."

"Foot? It's my knee that—have a look at my plow? What are you—"

"I think I heard someone mention in the village that they spotted you plowing and thought there was something amiss with the chain on the right," Jenny said as nonchalantly as possible.

Fine, so it was a lie. It wasn't a lie that Mr. Saunders was ever going to find out about, was he? She hadn't needed to see his plow to see he was compensating on his left for something wrong on the right.

Ten miles behind the plow to cover an acre. It was an awful lot of walking, and if there was a tug on one side with every step—

"Who's been gossiping about my plow?" Mr. Saunders said in a low voice, stepping toward her with a slight wince. "I won't have my plow talked about. I do an honest day's labor, without complaint—"

"I just thought I would mention it," Jenny said as brightly as possible.

And you're not going to listen, are you, she thought in exhaustion. *No, you're going to hold your head up high and assume there could not be anything wrong with your plow. And day after day, your knee is going to get worse and worse, until Mrs. Saunders is forced to take in laundry again.*

Why wouldn't these idiots just listen to her?

"Here," said Jenny softly, holding out a poultice which had taken her three days to make. "This is—"

"I don't need your pretended medicine!" shouted Mr. Saunders, pushing aside her hand so roughly the poultice fell to the floor with a soggy thump. "I didn't even want to come here and listen to your nonsense, but the wife—"

"Mr. Saunders, I am not forcing you to take the poultice," Jenny said softly, reaching down to pick it up.

She should be given a medal for speaking so calmly. There

was nothing so infuriating as a man who could be made well if he just put aside his prejudices and listened to her.

Time and time again, their wives would listen to her, and some of the more kindly men, like the vicar who was genuinely desperate due to pain in his hands. But men like Mr. Saunders? No, they came because they wished to escape the nagging. And when they came it was with bluster, rage, and embarrassment that they were pained at all.

It was exhausting.

"Force me to take that poultice, my eye!" spat Mr. Saunders. "You know it's true what they say about you, Miss Powell!"

Jenny's heart froze.

He had taken a step toward her—and he was so much taller than she was. Almost every man was in East Langdon, but she rarely had to worry about it.

She was worrying about it now. There was a bitter, unfriendly look in Mr. Saunders's face which she did not like.

"They say all sorts about you in the Red Lion," sneered the man. "And some of it true, I dare say! Why, you little—"

"I'd recommend you don't say another word, you cretin, before I do something you may regret," came quiet yet firm words.

Jenny gasped. She had not been aware of Moses moving from his armchair, but he had. Turning around to see him was unnecessary. She could feel him standing there, sense his presence, his chest just a few inches from her back. How had he moved so quickly? How could she tell he was so close, without even seeing him?

Mr. Saunders was still sneering. "Your charity case thinks he can protect you?"

Jenny's temper flared. "I did not think I would need protecting from an honorable resident of East Langdon, Mr. Saunders, and—Moses Warwick, put him down!"

It was not an order she ever thought she would have to give. Moses had growled as he moved, so rapidly it had happened in the blink of an eye. Mr. Saunders's ankles swung in the air as he was held inches from the floor by his collar.

His collar was in Moses's surprisingly strong grip.

"I think you were about to apologize to Doctor Powell," Moses growled. "Apologize, pay her a shilling for the poultice—"

"A shilling!" Jenny said in confusion.

It was all she could think to say. How could she address the far more challenging matter, which was that patients were not supposed to be manhandled and held aloft while threatened to pay money?

"—then you will thank the Doctor and be on your way," Moses continued to growl. "Do we understand each other?"

"I—wh—afsh—"

"Moses, he's struggling to breathe—put him down," ordered Jenny.

This was madness. A dream, surely. Dukes in disguise did not threaten her patients!

And yet it appeared one did. Slowly, Moses lowered the struggling man back to the ground. When he released his hand from Mr. Saunders's collar, the latter cleared his throat as he stumbled back.

"I—a shilling, right," Mr. Saunders said hurriedly after glancing at Moses. "Here."

Jenny stared as the man thrust a coin into her hand then immediately started backing away. Actually backing away, as though turning his back to them would only end in trouble.

"Mr. Saunders," she said weakly. "Your poultice—"

"Right, thank you, fine. Good day, Miss—Doctor Powell," Mr. Saunders amended hastily with a frightened look at Moses, poultice now clutched in hand.

And he was gone.

"Good riddance!" said Moses, turning to her with a smile. "You can thank—Jenny!"

Jenny thumped him hard, again, on the chest. It was rather satisfying to feel the thud of her fist hitting him. It allowed some of the anger she felt to seep out of her.

"What in God's name is that f—"

"How dare you!" Jenny said, blood boiling. *The nerve of the man!*

"How dare I?" repeated Moses, brow furrowed. "What, how dare I defend you? How dare I ensure you are actually paid for the hard work you put in? How dare I—"

"How dare you threaten someone in my home!" Jenny said, pulse thundering, pulse roaring in her ears. "How dare you coerce someone into giving me money—oh, I'll never live this down!"

The news would be all around the village by the evening. There wouldn't be a soul who hadn't heard how Miss Powell forced poor Mr. Saunders to hand over a coin, or else face violence from the ruffian who was living with her.

Living with her, and the two of them not married!

Jenny knew those would be the words next on everyone's lips. Oh, it had been a mistake to let Moses stay this long. She had told him to write to his friends, then his servants, but he had refused. Said he had not recovered.

Well, if he'd recovered enough to physically lift a man by his collar, he'd recovered enough to write a letter and go home.

"I thought you'd be grateful," Moses was saying hotly.

Jenny's eyes widened. "Grateful! Why on earth would you think that?"

"You cannot be serious."

"More serious than I have ever been in my life," Jenny said ardently, trying to keep her anger in check.

But she couldn't. It was all too much—having this duke here all the time, it was doing something strange to her mind, making it impossible to think clearly.

"You know what they say," said the infuriating man, a lazy smile slipping over his face. "A duke a day keeps the doctor away."

"And that's what you want, is it?" Jenny snapped. "To drive

away all my patients?"

It wasn't as though she earned a great deal from them, to be sure, but to lose them all . . .

He must have seen the exhausted look on her face. Moses's smile disappeared, guilt replacing it.

"I just tried to protect you," Moses said quietly, stepping toward her.

His increased proximity was not helping, but Jenny tried to speak calmly. "This is my home, and I have to be able to protect it and myself. It's not like you're going to . . . to be here forever!"

He was far too close now. Jenny could feel Moses's breath on her face, his scent filling her nostrils, making it almost impossible to think. Those sky-blue eyes were looking at her closely. As though he had never truly seen her before.

"Th-That's right, isn't it?" Jenny said, her voice breaking. "You're not going to be here forever. Are you?"

It was a foolish question. Perhaps if she had not been so riled by what had just happened with Mr. Saunders, she would not have even thought of asking it.

But she had asked now, and she could not bear to hear the reply. She already knew what it was.

Moses would leave. Not today, perhaps not even tomorrow. But a duke was not going to find a permanent home in West Cottage with a doctor routinely disrespected by those she regularly served, while he could be serving his country.

Yet Moses did not reply. Instead, he took another step toward her. Mere inches kept them apart. Jenny tried not to lean forward to feel the sensation of her breasts pressed up against him.

Was he looking at her differently? Or was she merely seeing what she wished to see?

"I can't stay forever," murmured Moses quietly.

Jenny nodded, biting back tears. She wasn't going to allow weakness. "I knew that."

"I did not intend to—"

"What's done is done," she said wearily. She couldn't stay

here—she had to get out. "I—I am going for a walk."

"Jenny—"

"I'll be back before dinner," Jenny said, pushing past him toward the door. She couldn't continue wallowing in the intoxicating presence of a man she would any day now be saying goodbye to. "Don't leave the cottage."

"Jenny—"

The door slammed behind her, and Jenny did not stop until she had walked hurriedly down the hall, grabbed a scarf from the hooks, and closed her front door.

Then she leaned against it.

What was she supposed to do with all these unbidden longings?

CHAPTER NINE

22 September 1811

"I'M BORED," MOSES announced to the air.

There was a snort just above him and to the side. He did not need to look to know who it was. There was usually only one person in West Cottage, and besides, he had long ago memorized the precise way Miss Jenny Powell snorted.

"You don't say," came her dry voice. "Does that explain why you're lying on my floor?"

It was a habit Moses had formed in childhood. A bad one, probably, but not one he had any interest in changing.

Whenever life grew too dull for words, he would find himself lying on his back on the floor, looking up at the ceiling. It calmed him in a way he could not explain. The pressing ache of being alone, unattended, and forced to make his own fun would fade away.

Sometimes he would look at the cracks in the ceiling of his schoolroom, up on the third floor of the manor house he spent his earliest years in. Sometimes he would attempt to name all the Greek gods in the pantheon painted on the ballroom ceiling. And sometimes he would just lie somewhere, eyes closed, until someone came and entertained him.

Strange. Moses had not indulged in the habit for quite some time. It was nice to know that the calming feeling still came when he needed it.

"Bored, bored, bored—"

"You know, you could just leave," Jenny's voice pointed out from where she was standing by the fire. "Don't you have a home to go to, Your Grace? Or several homes?"

Moses snorted. "I can't leave, not yet. I'm not fully healed."

It was a lie, and one he was almost certain Jenny knew full well was a lie.

Yet something kept him here. Despite knowing that he was probably needed back in France and that he most certainly should return to London to give his report—what he could remember of it—to Mr. Snee, Moses stayed.

He stayed in West Cottage, in East Langdon, in the middle of nowhere . . . with her.

Moses swallowed, shoulder tugging. Or not tugging. It had ceased to hurt a few days ago. At first he hadn't noticed, but it was impossible to ignore now.

"You are fully healed."

"But not fully rested," said Moses, unwilling to enter into the debate. "I'm staying for now, and that's final."

Another snort, one which made him smile.

Because he couldn't explain it. If Jenny sat him down and seriously asked why he had not made any move to leave, Moses could not tell her why. If she questioned him about his plans for the future, he could only honestly say he had none. And if she inquired why he had not let a single soul know he was here, safe and sound, when there would surely be an alarm raised by now . . .

Moses swallowed.

Well, he knew the answer, but he did not wish to give it.

The basic answer was simple. His memory had not completely returned. The precise reason why he had left France had not surfaced. Until he knew why, Moses could not tell whether he should go to London or France.

That was the official response and, if truly pressed, the one he would give Jenny.

But the whole truth?

Moses turned his head ever so slightly and watched the elegant woman lean over the fire, examining something in the pot that was bubbling above it.

Something else bubbled with similar heat.

How could he leave her? There was so much about Jenny he still did not understand, but every hour that went by he seemed to know her better. See more of her.

And he couldn't leave now. Not after he had been so foolish as to physically threaten a man just days ago.

"I think you were about to apologize to Doctor Powell."

Regret seared through Moses, though it was not the sort of regret Jenny would have approved of. Because it wasn't for the way he had spoken to Saunders he regretted, nor the way he had manhandled the arrogant brute into paying Jenny in actual coin.

No, it was for the fact he had done it in her presence. *What he should have done,* Moses thought darkly, *was follow the man out, push him against the wall, and tell him that unless he spoke to the doctor with some respect—*

"You'd have servants, you know," Jenny's voice said, cutting through his thoughts. "Waiting on you hand and foot. Wouldn't you prefer that?"

Moses grinned. "Why? You're doing that here for me already."

It was not quite true. She still did the cooking, but Moses had taken to carrying in logs for the fire, tidying the workroom as best he could. He'd even washed out a few glasses and beakers, though apparently he had done an insufficient job. Jenny had never asked him to repeat the task.

Jenny laughed bitterly. "Yes, I suppose I am. Is that why you stay, then? Because you like having someone's almost undivided attention?"

She glanced over through her lashes.

Moses's manhood twitched.

Nothing so innocent, he thought. *Not that I am about to admit that to you. I'm not sure I want to admit anything to you. Any weakness. Any thoughts I've had of you. The moments late at night when I can hear you moving about upstairs, and I wonder—*

"Something like that," Moses said, his voice somehow hoarse.

She laughed and he joined in with her merriment, though his heart skipped a beat as she stepped past him toward the table and her skirt brushed past his shoulder.

Dear God. He had never been so foolish about a woman before. What did he think he was doing?

Moses sat up. Lying on the floor wasn't helping, after all. How maddening.

Throwing himself into one of the armchairs, he looked over at Jenny and amused himself for a moment in watching her.

She was mixing medicines. How she knew what to do, he could not tell. Perhaps some of those books of hers, which she treated as though they were worth their weight in gold, contained the instructions.

No matter where she had gained the knowledge, it was clear Jenny knew precisely what she was doing. Moses watched, impressed beyond measure, as she moved surely around the table.

A handful of this, a smidge of that. The scales came out when it came to weighing the next ingredient, and there was a flask with quarter pint, half pint, three quarters pint, and pint marks up one side. All was mixed together with a pestle and mortar.

Even through the day gown, Moses could see the straining effort Jenny was putting in as she ground all the ingredients up together.

She was magnificent. Did she have any idea how unusual she was? How no one else was like her?

"You're watching me again."

"There's nothing else to do," Moses said expansively, throwing out his hands. "Nothing to entertain—"

"You could leave," Jenny said again more seriously, not turning to look at him. "There is always that option."

He swallowed. As yet, he had not had the bravery to ask her whether she wished for him to leave.

There were times . . . no, there were moments. Mere moments between them when he thought he saw something akin to friendliness in her expression when she beheld him. The rare times he made her laugh. When he caught a glimpse of her reading one of her favorite books, brow furrowed as she took in the words on the page.

Moses's stomach lurched. In those moments, he thought he would never leave.

And they had kissed.

Just the once. And she had slapped him soundly immediately afterward. A man could take a message from that.

Except he couldn't. Though Moses had not even thought of laying a hand on her skin—well, perhaps *thought* it—he would not cross that line again. He was a gentleman, even if he was a blackguard. And he would not touch a woman when she had made it so clear she had no wish for his caresses.

Moses's chest tightened. *Which was a shame.*

"Can I help?"

The words had not been what he had intended to say, and they surprised Moses just as much as they appeared to surprise her.

Pushing a curl back which had escaped its pins, Jenny stared. "You want to help?"

Apparently so, Moses thought wryly. Well, there was no point attempting to take it back now. "Yes. Why not?"

"You know, I'm not sure you can," said Jenny with a laugh. "It takes an intrepid mind to do this sort of thing. I don't know whether you're up to it."

Her laughter was quickly joined by his own and something eased in Moses.

There was something different about things between them. He had thought he'd lost all chance of gaining Jenny's trust after the . . . call it an altercation with Mr. Saunders. He had expected her to be impressed, to thank him. A small part of him had wondered whether he would be rewarded with a handshake.

Fine, a kiss.

But though Jenny had not thrown herself into his arms and declared that she could never live without him—just one of the daydreams Moses had permitted himself since then—she had been smiling more often.

Not something to be sneezed at.

"I want to be useful," Moses insisted, rising from his seat and walking over to the table. "You could put me to use—I can be helpful."

"Ah, but can you?" asked Jenny with a raised eyebrow as she delicately measured out a few drops of something from an amber bottle.

She laughed as she straightened up and saw Moses's expression. He could not keep his feelings hidden, but he hadn't thought it would be that amusing.

"I am very useful—and helpful!" he protested, picking up a jar of something gloopy that Jenny immediately took out of his hands. "I'll have you know I can be very . . . very . . ."

Words failed him as Jenny placed the jar on the table and put her hands on her hips.

How did she do that? Whenever she put her hands on her hips like that, and looked at him like that, as though . . .

As though you were a person she actually liked, Moses thought. *As though you amuse. As though you weren't a burdensome, weary excuse for a patient.*

He swallowed. "Very helpful."

Jenny shook her head ruefully. "I suppose it *might* be useful to have another pair of hands. If you can do what you're told."

Moses's heart leaped, just as he berated himself for thinking so much of this moment.

As soon as his memory had completely returned, he would be off. Back to London, or France, or wherever it was he was making for. His stay at West Cottage with Jenny would be nothing more than a memory. A waypoint in his journey, nothing more. He wouldn't be back.

The thought was painful. A jolt of agony crashed through his body, gone so swiftly that Moses gasped at its sudden arrival and departure.

It was wrong, the thought of leaving Jenny. And yet he would have to.

"Here," Jenny said, unaware of the tangled feelings he was wrestling with. "Chop these up into a fine powder."

Moses looked down at what she had pushed toward him. It was some sort of . . . root?

"A fine powder?" he repeated. *Dear God, he'd be here half the afternoon!*

She nodded. "Here, take this knife while I measure out the oil."

Nodding as though he perfectly understood why he was doing what he was doing, and why he had to wrench a knife through a knotted root continuously rather than—oh, pick petals off flowers—Moses took the knife she offered.

Then he looked down at the root. *Oh blast, he did have to open his fat mouth, didn't he?*

"So, tell me," Moses said quietly as he hacked none too gently at the root. "Why?"

"It's a rather useful root, actually," said Jenny, coming alive as she always did when she was speaking on something she knew a great deal about. "You see, the—"

"Not the root, you," he interrupted with a grin.

Her confidence faltered. "What do you mean?"

Moses gestured about the room. *Well, he'd wondered, and there seemed to be no better time to ask.* "All this. Your workroom, being a . . . treating people, like you do."

Why was it so impossible for him to call her a doctor? He had done when Mr. Saunders had been so rude to her.

"I think you were about to apologize to Doctor Powell."

The word had just slipped out before he could do anything about it. Moses had hoped Jenny had not noticed. She had not spoken of it since, but when it came to Jenny Powell, he was starting to learn that meant nothing. This was a woman who watched, who noticed things. She just didn't feel the need to speak about them.

Jenny seemed to know what he was thinking. "You mean, why did I want to become a doctor?"

Moses relented, despite his finer feelings. "Yes."

Yes. It was just a simple word, one which he rarely said to others. It was other people's responsibility to say yes to him, always had been. No one said "no" to a duke.

Except this woman, apparently.

Jenny did not answer at first. She was still looking carefully at the viscous liquid she was measuring, concentrating hard. It was only when she put it down, unmeasured, that Moses realized she had been weighing up something entirely different.

"My father," she said quietly. "He was sick."

He had intended this conversation to be a chance for her to share a little of her story. Perhaps for him to share a little of his. For the two of them to feel closer. Perhaps as he reached across the table their hands would meet . . .

Instead, he was clearly opening up old wounds. "I am sorry."

"It's not your fault," Jenny said bracingly. "You didn't make him sick."

If he could go back in time and make him well, Moses would. It was clear from the shadow of pain passing across the woman's face that the loss of her father, and he suspected at a young age, had changed her.

"I was certain if we could just find the right doctor, every-thing would be well," Jenny was saying with a false brightness that tore at Moses's heart. "But there wasn't a doctor to be found. Not one who would treat him, anyway. My father . . . well, I wouldn't call him a miser. Not to his face."

Moses grinned, then forced the grin away. *Not now, man!* "And so no one came?"

"He died three days later. A fever. I learned later how easily it could have been broken, healed," Jenny said in a brittle voice. Like it could shatter at any moment. "And I thought to myself at the time—I must only have been about eight or nine—I thought, one day, I will be a doctor. And I won't wait for people to hand over money before I treat them. I won't demand outrageous fees just to give someone the use of their arm back or to help a child through a sickness."

Guilt seared through Moses.

"Apologize, pay her a shilling for the poultice—"

Ah. Well, that would explain in part why Jenny had been so affronted by his demand that Saunders pay her a shilling. After suffering the loss of a parent due to a lack of money, a stubbornness of pride, he could see why she would react in precisely that way.

Blow it all to hell, no wonder she had done so. He'd prodded an old wound. One which apparently had not healed.

"It's unusual for a woman to wish for such a thing," he commented quietly.

"Keep going at that root."

Moses bit his tongue. His instinct to say he had no wish to chop up a root, but wanted to get to the root of who she was, would have impressed in London but would not wash here.

She was not the sort of woman to be dazzled like that.

"I just meant," he said as he returned to the root, "that—"

"I know what you meant," Jenny said quietly. "And I know how much I disappointed my mother by wishing such a thing."

There was pain in her words but also a complete absence of something Moses had expected to hear: regret.

"So you . . . you learned all this through books?" he hazarded.

Jenny rewarded him with a dry laugh. "Some of it is just common sense. You saw Mrs. Guernsey. You heard what I said to

Mr. Saunders, even if he did not wish to listen. His plow does tilt to the right, and it is putting pressure on his left leg. Even if he does not want to hear it."

Moses nodded, the root once again forgotten. How could he concentrate on a root when a woman like Jenny Powell was before him?

"And the books help," she continued, glancing over at her bookcase. "But it was my journey to Berlin that really—"

"I am sorry," said Moses, not at all sorry for interrupting. "You went to Berlin?"

There was something of a defiant glow in Jenny's eyes—one he knew well by now. "And why not? My mother thought I was going to a ladies' finishing school, but—"

"But you went to the university," declared Moses in awe.

Well, damn. She was far bolder than he had given her credit for. And she was trained, after a fashion. After accusing her of not having a whit of education, it was rather astonishing to discover she had sat and observed some of the finest medicine being practiced in Europe.

No wonder the people of East Langdon kept coming back to her. Why, Jenny Powell was probably one of the most educated women in the country.

"—and that was when the money ran out," Jenny said with a laugh. "I had to come home, and after a . . . well, let us call it a discussion with my mother, I came here. I serve the people of East Langdon, and I get by. And that's all I can ask for—the opportunity to serve and to be alone."

Moses swallowed.

They were not that different, after all. He had not missed the mention of a finishing school—she was a gentlewoman, even if she did live in a cottage in the middle of nowhere.

She had money, then. Or at least, she had done, once upon a time. Jenny could have lived a life of relative ease. Could have married a gentleman, or a man in trade if her family had been hard up. She could have been a wife and mother, and worried about nothing more serious than whether their neighbors had enjoyed the dinner she'd hosted the night before.

And instead she was here. Like him, having turned her back on a life of ease, she had chosen instead to serve.

"That root won't powder itself."

Moses started from his reverie.

Jenny had a knowing smile. "And you told me you could be helpful—"

"I can!" he said hastily, picking up his knife again. "I can impress—I mean, I want to impress you, Jenny."

Try as he might, Moses could not catch her gaze. Jenny was looking down at the handwritten instructions she was working from, and though her cheeks were pink, she did not look up.

"You can impress me, Moses," she said faintly, "by chopping that root into a powder."

CHAPTER TEN

30 September 1811

I T WAS ALL Jenny could do to remain standing on her feet, but she had no choice. The fire wasn't even lit, and she had at least four outstanding items on her to-do list.

That list will be the death of you, she thought, dropping her shawl onto an armchair and pulling off her fingerless gloves. *If the cold and infection doesn't get to you, the exhaustion will.*

"Goodness, it's cold out there!" declared Moses cheerfully, shivering as he stomped in after her. "And it's not remarkably warm in here. Shall I light a fire?"

Jenny looked around as she pulled her pencil from her hair, a quizzical lift of her brow her only response. *Light a fire?*

She'd never had anyone around to offer such a thing. Or even think of such a thing. Spending so much time alone in her own workroom had always felt like a privilege. Never having to worry about entertaining, never suffering the company of another for hours.

Yet somehow Moses's presence had gradually ceased to feel like a burden. It was almost as though he had become a part of the workroom itself.

Which, in a way, he had. Jenny supposed she should have

offered him the use of the only spare bedchamber upstairs, but somehow it had never crossed her mind. Anyway, she reasoned, Moses sleeping in the workroom was far better for him. And warmer overnight.

At least, when they had a fire going.

"Jenny?"

"Yes, yes, a fire," she replied hastily, stifling a yawn. "In both fireplaces, if you would."

"Cold?" Moses shot over his shoulder as he stepped toward the log pile.

Jenny stifled another yawn. *Really, she could do with a day off at some point, but who knew when that would come?* "Busy. I need to make up a few things."

"Now? It's past six o'clock. Isn't it time for dinner?" asked Moses cheerfully.

She shot him an irate look which was wasted on his back as he knelt over the fire. Just once, it would be nice if someone else offered to cook something for a change.

Until now there had only been her to cook for and care for on a daily basis. Jenny had never permitted anyone to stay in the workroom so long. They had never needed to. A particularly sick villager would not wish to stay with her, in any case. They would prefer to be in their own home, as was right. Yet Moses—

"I'm pretty certain I could cook you something," said Moses with a grin, glancing around as the kindling took and sparks flew up the chimney. "I've watched you do it, right? Let me cook for you—you're exhausted."

Jenny blinked. She was, and what was more, he had noticed.

Because he is around you absolutely all the time, muttered a dark voice within her mind. *Not because he was particularly looking at you. Or particularly concerned about you.*

This is a duke, Jenny! He was a spy—still could be, if he decides to return to that life.

And you're a doctor. You save lives, you don't take them or help others take them. Or fritter them away.

"No, it's quite all right," Jenny said decidedly, capturing a few loose curls and forcing them back into their pins. It was safer to be formal, to be aloof. "I have some broth to make anyway, so it will be easier if I just—"

"I can cut things up!" said Moses, springing to his feet like an eager spaniel. "I've got quite good at it, even you must admit!"

Jenny would not admit it. Partly because she did not think this man needed any praise, but mostly because his cutting skills were absolutely abysmal. She was running out of parsnips, too. She kept telling him they were roots needed for some of her medicines, but the man had obviously never seen a parsnip before, so he kept destroying them.

"Why don't you just sit there and keep out of the way?" she asked wearily.

The exuberance died in Moses's expression. "Oh. Oh, of—of course."

He folded himself into the armchair with a look of such disappointment, Jenny had to turn away and approach the table to prevent her conscience from prodding her into any rash decisions.

Well, she could let him do something, couldn't she?

No. Moses Warwick, Duke of Chetnole, was nothing more than a nuisance. She'd have less trouble if she'd taken in a stray dog, and that was saying something. What was it her father had always said?

"You have to stop taking in strays."

Jenny lifted the water pail and carried it to her cooking pot over the now roaring fire. He had been right. Her very nature was to offer room to those who needed it, and it did not always end well.

"What are you doing?"

She sighed. "Boiling water, Moses."

"I can—"

"You can do me a great service by sitting right there and doing nothing," Jenny said firmly with a warning glance.

Moses's smile was shy, somehow. *Shy? Moses?* "You don't like people, do you, Jenny?"

Her name on his lips made something within Jenny tighten, just for a moment. How long had it been since she'd had anyone around who called her by that name?

Though it had never caused the reaction she was feeling now. How did Moses somehow make her name, simple and unaffected, sound mysterious and desirable?

"I am not accustomed to people," she said shortly, when Moses continued to stare expectantly, waiting for an answer.

"But you care for people all the time," he pointed out.

Jenny shrugged as she returned to one of her cupboards and pulled out what she knew was there. Yes, in the cold store right at the back, a jar of onion peel, carrot ends, and two marrow bones. Perfect for broth.

"I-I find the presence of other people tiring," she said, hardly knowing why she was admitting this to a man who was the contrary, who could have no real understanding of what she meant. "It is easier for me to just remain—"

"But I'm here all the time now," Moses pointed out.

Jenny could not help it—she glanced over with a wry smile.

The man's face fell. "Oh. Oh! So my being here, it is constantly exhausting—"

"It's not personal," Jenny added hastily, hating how his expression had become so dour. "And honestly, sometimes I hardly notice you."

She had intended the words as a compliment. She laughed as she watched Moses's shoulders droop even farther.

"It's a good sign," she said softly, dropping the contents of the jar into the now boiling water. "I promise. When . . . I mean, it happens rarely that I become so comfortable with someone that I can relax just as though they are not there. It's . . . it's rare."

Despite every instinct within her that told her this line of conversation was dangerous, Jenny met his eyes.

Moses's dour expression was gone. Instead, there were two pink dots on his cheeks and a lopsided grin across his lips.

Jenny immediately looked away. She wasn't staring at a handsome man who had been living with her now for weeks, noticing just how delightful his lips were. Definitely not.

"Oh," said Moses softly.

Jenny swallowed. "Yes. It's a compliment, as I said."

"Yes, I can see that," he said, his voice still low. "Thank you. For telling me, I mean. You cannot know how much that means to me."

There was such sentiment in his words, such fervor in his tone, Jenny could not help looking up from the potatoes she was now slicing to meet his eye again.

Was he thinking about it too? The kiss? The way he had so easily pulled her into his arms? The connection of their lips, the way desire had sparked in her—surely he had known? The instant it felt right, perfect, their intimacy a natural feeling between them?

"And you never will again."

Jenny swallowed. She had said those words and meant them. At the time.

Now . . .

Well. She could hardly go about asking a duke for a kiss, now could she? It would be most uncouth! And while he did not know precisely what sort of a lady she was, she certainly wasn't *that* sort.

"So," Moses said bracingly, breaking the moment. "What are you making? Dinner, I hope."

Jenny looked quickly at the knife and vegetables on the table. "Dinner for us, broth for a few families."

"A few—Jenny Powell, you're not attempting to make dinner for the whole village, are you?"

She noticed his teasing tone and tried to ignore the delightful swooping sensation in her stomach. "No, not quite. It's just broth."

"But it's not for us?"

"I didn't think you would be satisfied with broth," Jenny shot back, trying to match the lightness of his tone. She could keep up with him just as well, as long as—

"Oh, there's a great deal about you I think would satisfy," came Moses's low words.

Jenny dropped her knife.

"I said, there's a great deal about your cooking I think would satisfy," Moses repeated, louder this time.

Her cheeks were burning as Jenny reached for the knife which had only just missed her foot. Of course that was what he said—of course! She had misheard, that was all.

You are getting yourself tangled in something unbecoming of you, Jenny Powell, she thought sternly. *Seeing things that aren't there. Longing for things—*

Honestly! This had gone far enough!

"For a few families," said Moses, in a more conversational tone than before. "Why?"

That was it—focus on the medicine. That was what she knew. Not dukes, nor spies, nor danger. Medicine.

"Half the ailments in East Langdon are due to lack of food," she said, concentrating on the vegetables before her. "Without sufficient food and a wide variety of it, villagers are wont to succumb to all sorts of things."

"A wide variety?" Moses sounded skeptical. "And this to be found in East Langdon?"

Jenny pushed a curl out of her eyes and smiled. Merely because she was being polite. Not because she wanted to smile. "I think you'd be surprised at the variety of fruit and vegetables grown in people's gardens. The river isn't too far, and there's trout and salmon in the spring and eels. Most families raise a pig for Christmas—"

"And I suppose the woodlands nearby provide chestnuts and berries?" Moses said innocently.

Jenny frowned. "You are teasing me."

"It just sounds rather idyllic, that's all," he shrugged.

"A little different from food being brought to your table on a silver platter?"

She had not intended to tease. The words had slipped out before she could readily halt them, but that did not explain why Jenny had spoken them with a laughing air.

Moses matched her merriment. "Yes, I suppose so—but I did live off the land in France, you know. Mostly."

Jenny laughed. "You mean, you stole from whoever was about."

"Stealing is such a harsh word," Moses interrupted with a grin. "I repaid whenever I could, though I admit it was not always. But anyway, I was fighting the French! I couldn't sit there and worry about a few missing eggs!"

"And I suppose when you return to your London townhouse, or your ducal manor," said Jenny, her stomach swooping, "you'll have whatever you want on a plate, will you?"

And somehow the innocent laughter they had been sharing changed into something else. Something more suggestive and altogether more intoxicating.

Whatever he wants on a plate.

Well, he could forget that for a start, Jenny thought as she saw the way Moses's attention meandered. She wasn't some harlot presenting herself to a duke just because he asked for it!

Not that he *had* asked for it. If he did . . .

Jenny swallowed, but could not forget the image that had burst, unbidden, into her mind. An image of herself and Moses. Close. Closer than close. Her in his arms, and his lips on hers, and suddenly there weren't any clothes and—

"You do too much."

Jenny's eyes snapped open. *Oh, God, when had she closed them?* "I beg your pardon?"

She carried the chopped vegetables to the cooking pot in an attempt to distract herself, to think of the broth she was making, and not the delectable duke just a few feet away.

"For East Langdon. For everyone in it, you do too much," Moses said firmly. "Where's the nearest lord—can't he do something? Feed families and all that?"

Jenny snorted, then covered her mouth with her hand to prevent a cough.

Well, it wouldn't do any good to actually tell him, would it? That was too complicated a story. And nothing good could come of it. He'd only misunderstand.

"I do what I can," she said, after returning to the safety of the table.

Strange. It was only a few feet farther than the fires, yet somehow she felt encircled by it. It gave her the sense Moses could not reach her here. Even if it was not true.

Glancing up, Jenny's insides burned with the look he was giving her.

Definitely not true.

"I just don't understand how you can do all this," Moses said quietly.

Jenny shrugged, though her bones were weary. It was a question she had asked herself . . . was it last winter? And she had decided, no matter what, to stay. These people needed her. And it was nice, in a way, to be needed.

"Oh, easily enough. The broth is not complicated, and I use—"

"I mean, wearing yourself thin serving others," he interjected with a look that was all too knowing. "Spending money you don't have, scraping a living and receiving no payment. And you knew precisely that's what I meant, Jenny."

Hearing her name on his lips was intoxicating. This was why Society did not permit such intimacies. Because it could all of a sudden lead to—

"I get by," she said, as airily as possible.

The truth wasn't something he wanted to hear. Nor was it something she particularly wanted to tell.

There was far too much water under the bridge to explain it all, and besides, that part of her life was over. She would never go back—and he wouldn't understand that. Moses may even try to do something daft and noble and attempt to send her back.

"Jenny—"

"People pay me as they can, and I help them," she said, more sternly than she had intended. "I suppose a duke may not understand that. Your steward however—"

"I have always maintained good oversight of my estate's accounts, and you are avoiding the question," Moses said with a laugh, getting up and walking over to her.

Every step he grew closer, the room warmed. Or was that just her imagination? Was it possible it was not the room that warmed, but herself?

Jenny swallowed and hated that her voice faltered as he reached the table. "I-I . . . I don't have to explain—"

"Because I have not seen a single person pay you," Moses said gently, slipping onto one of the chairs and staring up without a waver. "Except for that Saunders, and—"

"You should not have done that," Jenny said in a low voice.

Her stomach tied itself into a knot as she recalled that moment. She had to hope the news had not spread too far—that Mr. Saunders had been so embarrassed, that he had not wished to make it known.

"You deserve payment, Jenny." Moses's voice was low, urgent. "You are highly skilled at your work, you . . . you heal people. Do you not think you deserve remuneration?"

Jenny stared.

Strange. Somehow, his approval of her and her work meant something to her.

She had never been one for seeking the approbation of others. Ladies did not, as a general rule, nor did they have the opportunity—at least not in personal or professional pursuits. The expectation was to marry and birth heirs, and that was about it.

So why did it spark such joy to hear Moses speak so well of her? Why did his interest in her intrigue her so? And why was she regretting, more and more with each passing moment, that she had told Moses never to kiss her again?

"Why do you care?" Jenny breathed.

Moses looked taken aback. "I-I . . . I don't know."

Jenny knew that if she spoke now, she would say something she would regret. Some sort of honesty would pour from her lips, dangerous indeed.

Honesty like: *Stay here, with me. Forever.*

Like: *You're the first person in the world I can stand to spend more than an hour with.*

Like: *When you kissed me, you thought I stopped the kiss because I didn't like it, but I stopped it because I liked it too much. Because I didn't want you to stop. Because I could have kissed you all day, and . . .*

Jenny swallowed. "When did . . . did you say you were going?"

And the moment, whatever it was that they were sharing ended abruptly.

Moses looked away. "I didn't."

"But—"

"I haven't yet retrieved all my memory, Jenny," he said, a harshness in his voice she had not expected. "I don't—I can't recall . . ."

His voice trailed away, and a look of earnest vulnerability covered his face. It was so fragile, Jenny's eyes widened.

What must it be like, to have a part of you missing because you could not remember something important? Rather like having your right hand cut off, she supposed. Or losing one's sight. Not impossible to adapt to, but startlingly painful and shocking, nonetheless.

"How can I serve my country if I don't even remember what I was trying to do in returning?" he asked, his voice cracking. "What use am I? A duke with no real skills, a spy who cannot keep a secret. What will the point of me be, Jenny?"

Instantly Moses's face changed, his expression becoming more wooden. Obviously he believed he had said too much. Perhaps he had.

"And . . ." Jenny swallowed, hating how her voice was so

weak. "And you will stay, then, until—until you have remem-bered?"

She had not intended to meet his gaze—that was far too dangerous at the moment.

She did so anyway. Moses's light blue eyes were like the sky on a midwinter morning, frost on the ground and breath billowing before him. Cold, crisp, with the promise of comfort soon to come.

"I will leave when I remember why I left France," he said quietly. "And not before. Now, how can I help with this broth of yours?"

CHAPTER ELEVEN

1 October 1811

I T WAS THE scream that did it.

There was something about a scream. Moses had never known until he'd gone to France, but there are very few things that can immediately wake you up from a deep sleep, if you are fortunate enough to slip into one. A scream is one of them.

"Jenny?" Moses said reflexively, jerking awake the moment the scream entered his skull.

There was silence and stillness. Nothing moved in the workroom. It had seemed a very strange place in the dark when he had first come out of his fever, but now Moses was so accustomed to it, it almost—

Another scream.

Moses bolted from the bed to the door and into the corridor.

He had never precisely been banned from going upstairs. It had simply never been discussed. It never had to be. Upstairs was Jenny's domain: her refuge from the world when socializing with him grew too wearisome. It was where she slept.

Moses's stomach lurched. He did not have time to think about Jenny in a nightgown, moonlight drifting behind her, a welcome patch in her bed just waiting for him—

"Jenny?" he called up the staircase.

Heart thundering, Moses tried desperately to think what to do as he brushed sleep from his eyes. If Jenny was hurt, if the pain was so exquisite she was screaming, surely she would not mind if he—

The loud banging made him jump, but once again his instincts took over. Moses stepped over to the front door and wrenched it open.

The screaming returned, and louder, and Moses looked into the eyes of a man who looked terrified. He was holding a small girl. The girl was the one screaming.

"Help me!" cried the man in a piteous voice.

Moses just stood there, transfixed. Never before had he been faced with such a situation, and he could barely take in what he was seeing. There was blood, blood everywhere, and screaming, and the man's cheeks were wet with tears, and he didn't know what to do—

"Move—move, Moses!"

Strong hands grabbed his arms and pulled him aside.

It was Jenny. She was wearing a nightgown, but sadly not the sort that featured regularly in Moses's dreams. It was thick, and woolen, and was covered by a gentleman's dressing gown which made no sense in his confused mind.

But most importantly, it was being worn by Jenny—and Jenny knew what to do.

"This way, Mr. Hodgson, and hurry—Moses, a fire, matches, candles, light," ordered Jenny in a firm voice as she strode along the corridor to her workroom. "Quickly!"

Moses wasn't certain whether the indictment for haste was for his benefit or the man's. Both ran after her.

The floor around the table was chaos. Books, papers, pens, ends of vegetables, a wooden box—all must have been swept off the table by the calm and controlled Jenny.

"Lay her on the table, Mr. Hodgson, and let's see what we're working with," she instructed calmly. "Come on, let me help you with her. Moses, light."

Moses blinked. "What?"

His pulse was racing, his lungs were tight, and he could barely tell what she was saying.

The girl was utterly covered in blood, the man's distress so evident, the screams . . .

Nothing in France could have prepared him for this. He had been a spy, not a solider. He had never killed, nor seen a man killed before him. He had worked in secret, and on secrets, and within secrecy. He had never seen anything like this.

Jenny's face appeared before him as the rest of the workroom blurred. "Moses? Moses, I need you to light a fire in the grate. Can you do that for me?"

Moses blinked and her face sharpened in his vision. A fire. Jenny needed him to light a fire. "Y-Yes, I can—"

"Thank you," Jenny murmured, reaching over and squeezing his hand.

And it was that small amount of contact that did it. Or perhaps her thanks, the way she had breathed it, not said it. As though she were depending on him.

Moses straightened up. *She was depending on him.*

Trying to blot out the moans from the small bundle of life now lying on the table, he rushed forward and within a minute, had a fire going in the grate. It warmed him, pumping warmth through his bones.

"Candles, Moses." Jenny's order came from the table, and as he looked around for the blasted things, she added, "Top drawer, cupboard nearest the door. Now then, my dear, let's take a look . . ."

The man, who Moses assumed was the girl's father, was sobbing as he sat in an armchair. Moses ran past him to the cupboard, wrenched open the top drawer, and found a plethora of candles. He put both hands inside, grabbed as many as he was able, and hurried them over to the table.

"Candles," Moses said confidently, averting his eyes from the child.

Jenny nodded. "Excellent, thank you, Moses. Do you think you can light them for me?"

He looked down at the candles in his hands, then back up at her, then at the candles. *Damn and blast it, he was supposed to be the gentleman, the spy, the duke! He wasn't supposed to be letting Jenny take the burden of all this!*

"Right, light," he said vaguely. "Around the table?"

"As close as you can get without burning this little one," Jenny said, stroking the girl's hair. "And I need the leatherbound kit in the second drawer down. Which drawer?"

But Moses could not answer. His gaze had been pulled, despite himself, to the child. *Oh, God, there was so much—*

"Moses—Moses!" Jenny said urgently, cupping his cheek and lifting his head. "Which drawer?"

He could hardly draw breath, there was such panic in his lungs. *How did she do it? How did she stay so calm and so unruffled?*

"S-Second," he managed. "I'll light these candles now . . ."

How he did it, Moses was not sure. When he looked back, he had no conscious memory of doing so. Despite his panic, the workroom grew lighter and lighter. As Mr. Hodgson continued to sob, Jenny leaned over his daughter and as far as Moses could see, did nothing immediately but gently wash away the blood.

By the time Moses had grabbed the leather whatever-it-was from the second drawer and brought it over to Jenny, the scene was much more palatable.

The child had a nasty gash down her leg. It looked horribly painful, jagged even. But there was just one.

Jenny smiled, dark circles under her eyes, as Moses offered the leather thing. "Thank you. Can you hold a candle close without letting wax drop? I need every bit of light you can muster."

Moses did not have to think. He could not doubt her now.

"I am the doctor, you idiot."

None of her arguments, their discussions, their debates were as convincing as this. He had been around doctors before, seen what happened to Wincham when a doctor finally caught up with him. There was a calmness about doctors that had to be trained.

And Jenny had it.

"Everything is going to be all right," Moses found himself saying as he held not one, but two candles close to the girl's leg.

"There, you see? My friend, Mr. Warwick, is absolutely certain things will be fine," said Jenny soothingly to the child, who managed a weak smile. "I'm going to sew you up—"

"I beg your pardon?" interrupted Moses, unable to help himself.

Sew her up? A memory, a flash of pain. Wincham.

Moses swallowed. It was a dark and difficult business, the sharp end of medicine.

Jenny was frowning and Moses immediately put aside all thoughts of interrupting again. "As I said, I'm going to sew you up, then give you a special drink to help you sleep. Are you ready, Gladys?"

The girl nodded, though Moses hardly knew why. When Jenny opened up the leather kit, there were needles and knives and all sorts of sharp, painful-looking instruments.

"Closer with that candle, please, Moses."

He nodded, obeying rather than trying to explain what he had been distracted by. Jenny would hardly be impressed.

And wanting to impress Jenny Powell was starting to become a hazard of being around her for too long, Moses was finding. It was not a common occurrence for him. Few people had characteristics he wished for, and most of the time, he was happy just being himself without any extra effort.

But with Jenny? This Jenny, who served people without question, without expectation of payment? Who used her own food to feed the village, who was woken in the dead of night by a screaming child and merely started to heal?

Moses's heart skipped a beat as he watched Jenny skillfully

knit the wound together, the stitches quick and neat, causing as little pain as possible.

She was a marvel. This woman could do anything, he was certain, anything she put her mind to. It was probably a good thing she had decided to be a doctor and not a politician. The world as he knew it would have been irrevocably changed.

If it wasn't already.

"There we go," said Jenny with a smile for the child, sadly not for him. "Now then, Mr. Warwick is going to stay with you just for a moment—"

"Doctor Powell—"

"Just for a moment," Jenny continued steadily, squeezing the girl's hand. "I need to go and get your medicine. I'll be right back. Thank you, Mr. Warwick."

Moses's stomach lurched. "Jenny—"

But it was too late. She had walked over to one of her innumerable cupboards, rummaging for something.

The girl she had called Gladys looked up, cheeks tearstained, but even so a hint of curiosity in her eyes. "You're new to the village."

Moses swallowed. Her father's sobs had receded. Perhaps he could—

"Mr. Warwick is a silly name," Gladys pronounced decidedly.

He could not help but smile. "It is, rather."

"But I s'pose you don't get to pick your name," the little girl continued, exhaustion evidently allowing her tongue to loosen. "If I could of chosen my name, I would of—"

"Could *have*, Gladys," Jenny called out across the room.

The girl frowned. "Could have, then, an' all."

Moses's smile broadened. "What would you have chosen?"

How resilient children were. He had never thought about it much, but he certainly would not have happily chatted away to a stranger about the name he would have chosen for himself if his own leg had been gashed open and freshly sewn up.

By the time Jenny returned with a mug of something that

looked distinctly like redcurrant wine, Moses had discovered Gladys had a chicken of her own, a favorite book he was almost certain was a hymnal, and she would much rather have been called Cordelia.

"Drink this down you, Cordelia," said Jenny resolutely, helping the girl to lift her head.

Moses watched with a strange glow as the child brightened up.

"You called me Cordelia! This has lavender in it, doesn't it? And honey, and what my Granny calls special tonic. You can't call me Cordelia!"

"I suppose not, though you're almost old enough to make up your own mind about things," said Jenny, glancing over her shoulder and jerking her head at the waiting father, who strode over. "But in the meantime, until you are old enough, I need you to promise me three things."

Moses stifled a laugh as Mr. Hodgson pushed him aside to get closer to his daughter.

"Firstly, no more climbing in the barn when someone leaves a sickle in there," Jenny said sternly. "Secondly, your name will be Gladys until you're old enough to change it yourself."

The girl considered this for a moment. Moses almost laughed. *The boldness of youth.*

"And thirdly," Jenny said sternly, "I would like you to come back and see me when you're all mended and we'll see if you've got a nose for some other herbs, if your parents will allow it."

The two of them looked at Mr. Hodgson. Moses could see he had been put into a corner. The last thing he could do, his child happy and on the road to recovery thanks to this woman waiting for a response with an arched eyebrow, was refuse permission for something so innocent.

"Y-Yes," he stammered. "As long as her mother agrees."

"Well then!" said Jenny. "Mr. Hodgson, if you would carry Gladys over to the pallet by the fire—you don't mind giving up your bed, do you, Mr. Warwick?"

As if he could refuse her either. He saw a twinkle in her eye that showed him she knew precisely what he was thinking. "Of course."

"And then you should get off home, Mr. Hodgson, and sleep well in your own bed," Jenny said.

"Oh, but—"

"I will stay up with her," continued Jenny with another stern look. "But you need your rest. The last of the harvest won't be brought in by an exhausted man."

There was something about the direct way Jenny had with people. She wasn't exactly rude, but it wasn't far off.

Still, it got results. Within another five minutes, Gladys was settled in his bed, Mr. Hodgson had gone, and he and Jenny were sat in the armchairs watching the girl sleep.

"What did you put in the drink?"

Jenny grinned. "Mead, lavender, a little laudanum for the pain, and a great dollop of whiskey for sleep. She'll be out or groggy for at least twelve hours, I think."

Moses stared, transfixed. How could anyone compare to this woman? How had he ever thought that she was unfit to call herself a doctor?

"You did well," he said quietly. "And you'll be training her up, I suppose."

Even in the gloom of the night, with only a few candles still lit on the table, he could see Jenny flush. "I merely did what anyone—"

"I thought I was good in a crisis, and you were running rings around me," Moses admitted with a wry smile. "I've never seen a child—I mean, all that blood—"

"The first time is always the worst," Jenny said softly, her eyes drifting over to the sleeping child. "But sadly, those sorts of accidents happen more often than you would think. You just have to be prepared."

As she was. Everything was ready, and she had known precisely where everything was kept. It was impossible not to be impressed—and for the first time, Moses knew he could not keep his admiration to himself.

Jenny Powell deserved to know how impressive she was.

"You were magnificent," Moses said. "No, do not attempt to say you were not. We both know the truth."

There was a rather shameful look on her face which simply did not make any sense. "I only did what anyone else would—"

"I would have fair panicked, and that would have been about it." Moses shifted ruefully in his armchair. *If only the two were closer . . .* "You saved that child's life."

Jenny waved a hand. "I only—"

"If the blood loss hadn't done it, an infection in a poorly tended wound that size would have killed a child like that, and you know it," Moses said quietly. "Do you think her father will ever know what you did for them?"

He watched her hesitate. Had watched the war within her. He could see the desire to be kind and polite to the man who had done naught wrong but leave a tool of his trade in a barn, where he had thought it safe. That desire battled with another truth, which was that the Hodgson family would never know that, but for Jenny's quick thinking, their numbers would have been down by one this Christmas.

"I am sure they are grateful," Jenny said eventually.

Moses's lungs tightened. "You are a truly talented doctor."

There. It was said. He should have said it a while ago, but he hadn't been able to bring himself to do it. No man liked to admit that he was wrong. A gentleman liked it even less, and a duke? Dukes never admitted anything. At least, Moses had never been in the presence of an apologizing duke, and he knew a fair few.

But he had said it—and more importantly, he had managed to hold Jenny's gaze while he did so. And that meant Moses was rewarded by the sight of not only a Jenny who was delighted by his words, but also one who was . . .

Was that a flush on her cheeks? Was he imagining it, or was there a throb at her neck, her pulse quickening? Was it possible that she was feeling the effect she had on him every day?

"It took a great deal for you to admit that," Jenny said softly, "didn't it?"

Moses blew out his cheeks. "Yes."

Her laughter was light, unlikely to wake the sleeping child but loud enough for him to hear. "Well, thank you."

"I do not think you need to thank me," said Moses, wishing he knew what to do with his hands. *What did people do with their hands, anyway?* "In truth, I think I need to be asking for your forgiveness."

He could not deny it any longer. The admiration he had for Jenny was not merely for her skill and compassion as a doctor, though that was great. No, it was for her beauty. Her mind. Her elegance. The way that she leaned over a cooking pot on the fire, the instinct to help anyone, regardless of whether they could reciprocate.

Jenny was starting to bewitch him. If he were not careful, he would find himself unable to leave.

"I will leave when I remember why I left France. And not before."

Moses had meant it when he had said those words. But there was more to his intention now. How could he leave East Langdon, West Cottage, when he had still not gained a full understanding of the complex and beautiful woman before him?

"Forgiveness?" Jenny murmured. "I am not sure about that."

"I certainly have not treated you with the respect you deserve," Moses said, hating that he had to remind her of the inexcusable behavior she had suffered from him. "And for that I am truly sorry."

She met his eye, then smiled as she offered out her hand. "You are forgiven."

Moses had only intended to take it to show Jenny how grateful he was for her forgiveness. It was not a given, he knew, and there was nothing he wished for more than her mercy in that moment.

The instant their hands touched, however, he wanted something much more. To feel the softness of her skin, hold her hand, feel her pulse. To know her to be his. To hear her ask, this time, for a kiss she would welcome. For the sensation of her under him, squirming, begging him to—

"Well, I don't know whether you're going to get any sleep in that armchair," said Jenny, pulling her hand from his. "I'll be remaining awake to keep an eye on Gladys, but you—"

"I'll stay up with you," Moses found himself saying, even as his head ached with tiredness.

Jenny frowned. "You will?"

He nodded and said the words that he should probably only have thought. "Anything to spend more time with you."

CHAPTER TWELVE

4 October 1811

"—AND IF IT starts to itch again, you absolutely must tell me," Jenny said, in her best severe voice. "I mean it, Mrs. Peters!"

"Yes, yes, thank you dear," said the old woman from her armchair by the fire. "I'm sure I will think about—"

"You heard the doctor, Mrs. Peters," said Moses in that low, calming voice he had. "As soon as it starts to itch."

Jenny did her best not to roll her eyes as the older woman fluttered her eyelashes at the tall, handsome duke.

Not that she knew Moses Warwick was a duke. Old Mrs. Peters would likely as not have had a fit if she knew the dashing gentleman who had carried her up to her bed was in fact the Duke of Chetnole.

"Oh, if you say so, Mr. Warwick," said Mrs. Peters cheerfully. "And I must say, it is so nice for you to be helping Doctor Powell. You've needed an extra pair of hands for a while, haven't you, dear?"

Jenny's smile faltered, but only slightly.

She knew what they were thinking. The whole village would be thinking it by now. It had been, after all, over a month since "Mr. Warwick" had started living in her cottage.

Anyone who asked had been told the truth: that the man was still recovering from a terrible fever, and that he was sleeping soundly in the temporary bed in her workroom.

She didn't need to add that he was a duke. Or that he had been stabbed in the back, something she had still not yet had the courage to ask him about. Or that she had been tempted, after they had cared for little Gladys, to invite him up to her own bed and show him, not tell him, just how grateful she was that . . .

"Doctor Powell?"

Jenny shook her head, as though that would help her concentrate. She needed to focus. The last thing she needed was for people to get the wrong idea about her and Moses!

Her and Mr. Warwick, that was.

Her and the Duke of Chetnole.

Oh Lord . . .

"So we're agreed then, Mrs. Peters," Jenny said aloud in an attempt to focus on what was before her. "Any itching—"

"And I'll have one of my boys sent round to you," said Mrs. Peters with a sigh. "And . . . and you will come too, won't you, Mr. Warwick?"

"You're starting to get admirers," Jenny said with a grin as they stepped out of Mrs. Peters's cottage ten minutes later, after she had managed to extricate him from the woman.

Moses shrugged, though there was discomfort in his eyes. "Oh, I am sure she is just being polite—"

"I wouldn't count on it," said Jenny, heaving her basket back onto her arm as they started along the lane to the next house on her list. "Mrs. Peters lost her husband two winters back, but I don't think she would be averse to finding another."

It was all she could do not to look up into Moses's face as she spoke. She hadn't actually asked the question aloud, even if she had thought it with every fiber of her being . . .

"Marriage," Moses said confidently, "is not something I am interested in. And certainly not with Mrs. Peters. No offense meant, naturally."

Jenny wasn't certain if it was relief or disappointment rushing through her veins. It was certainly something, a heady, giddy sensation that made it difficult to concentrate on where she was going. She almost—

"Careful!" Moses grabbed her arm as Jenny's foot slipped on the muddy path. "Here, let me take that. It's far too heavy for you, anyway."

"I can manage—"

"I didn't say you couldn't," said Moses evenly, taking the basket from her arm, nonetheless. "Merely that I wanted to help."

Jenny opened her mouth to argue, but it was pleasant not to have the heavy weight on her arm. And he hadn't said she was unable to cope with it.

It was a strange feeling, being helped. Typically, she was the one doing the helping, not accepting the help. It was difficult, now she came to think about it. How did everyone else manage it?

And he had been helpful.

Oh, Moses was never going to make a doctor. He wouldn't make a good nurse, either. He had no head for the gory bits of doctoring, and he still couldn't tell a carrot from a parsnip, though he had finally cottoned on to the fact she was giving him vegetables to destroy—that was to say, chop—rather than any herbs she intended to use in one of her concoctions.

But he had been helpful. Chopping wood yesterday—Jenny had managed to watch him, shoulders straining, muscles bulging through his shirt, for only five minutes.

It was a long five minutes. A warm one. But no more than that.

He'd also got into the habit of laying the fire every morning, which was a great help. And he brought in water from her well in the afternoon. And he . . .

Jenny wasn't certain what she was going to do without him, in truth. When he left.

Her stomach lurched as her foot slipped once more.

"Here, take my arm," said Moses, not waiting for her to accept or argue, but instead taking her hand and placing it on his arm.

It was done so smoothly, so without conscious thought, Jenny rather thought she saw a flush come over his cheeks as he realized what he had done. She watched Moses's jaw tighten, then relax.

What did it mean?

Oh, Jenny knew the signs and symptoms of a myriad of diseases. She knew when an injury was going bad and what to do with a broken bone. She even had a few ideas about curing the cold, which all her books told her was nigh on impossible. But this?

Lovesick, Jenny thought ruefully.

She could diagnose it in herself, even if she did not like it. But that was because she knew herself. What love, or lovesickness, looked like in other people? That was something she simply could not understand.

Did he . . . care about her?

"Is that better?" Moses asked quietly.

She was so close to him, her arm tucked into his, that Jenny could feel the thrum of his words in him. She nodded, rather than risk her voice.

Yes, it was better. And after they visited the Hodgsons and ensured Gladys was healing up as well as could be expected, neither Moses nor Jenny said a word as she slipped her hand again into his arm when they returned to the lane.

This was . . . a habit, Jenny thought sternly. *That was all. It didn't mean anything.*

But what was love, if not habit? The habit of seeing each other and being comfortable with each other—and no one else. Creating a routine in a home you shared, and laughing together, and wanting to be close . . .

Jenny swallowed and set her jaw. She was not going to fall in love. She had far more important things to worry about.

"Where next?"

She glanced up and her heart skipped a beat as tingles of pleasure flickered across her collarbone toward her breasts.

This was ridiculous. She needed to get this duke out of her system, one way or another! After all, it was not as though he was thinking these ridiculous thoughts, too.

"Just Mrs. Guernsey," she said aloud. "I hope she's still been heeding my words not to knit over the fire . . ."

She had not. Jenny sighed and shook her head, slipping her hand from Moses's as she stepped inside. "Mrs. Guernsey, I told you—"

"I know, I know," said the older woman, wringing her hands. "And I knew you'd carry on like this, but I have to work, Doctor Powell!"

Jenny softened as the door closed behind her and she took in the shabby state of Mrs. Guernsey's cottage.

Poverty was not something one had, but what one slipped into. You were doing fine and then before you knew it, you were behind on a few things, and you bought less fuel for your fire, and a little less meat. And then no meat, and your clothes were mended never replaced, and there was no need for a fire in September, was there?

And before you knew it, you were poor.

Jenny sighed. "Let's have a look."

Heartily conscious of Moses's presence as she examined the poor woman's eyes, Jenny cast about for something for the man to do.

"Do you have any chores needing doing, Mrs. Guernsey?"

Mrs. Guernsey blinked. "Chores?"

Jenny nodded, trying to tilt the woman's head back to get light into her eyes. "Mr. Warwick here is in urgent need of employment and would be more than happy to—"

"Jenny," hissed Moses.

She could not help but grin. "Some logs that need chopping, perhaps?"

Mrs. Guernsey's expression changed. "Why, it would be a great help!"

Jenny's grin broadened as Moses cast her a look then bowed at the nearsighted Mrs. Guernsey. "It would be my pleasure, madam."

It was a wonder she had not guessed at the man being nobility, Jenny thought as she showed Mrs. Guernsey how to wash out her eyes with just a small amount of water. The way he spoke sometimes, it was uncanny.

"Your young man is doing an excellent job," said Mrs. Guernsey conversationally.

"He's not my young man, Mrs. Guernsey," Jenny replied as she handed the woman back her spectacles.

The older woman's eyes glittered. "Isn't he?"

With a jerk of the head, she indicated something behind Jenny.

Jenny turned, and she gasped involuntarily.

Well, he was rather splendid. Despite the cool of the day, Moses had taken off his new—or rather, old—jacket and hung it on a fence post. The ax in his hands gleamed in the frosty autumnal sun, and when he swung it—

Jenny shivered.

"Just because I like the look of a man—" she began stiffly.

Mrs. Guernsey giggled. "No harm in looking, I suppose."

No harm in looking. Those were the words racing about Jenny's mind as she and Moses, jacket now returned to its proper place, bid Mrs. Guernsey farewell and started on the walk back to West Cottage.

No harm in looking. Except there was, wasn't there? Jenny was no stranger to the theories of attraction. There were some practicalities of birth and labor—and what led to them—she'd learned early on when sitting in on lectures in Berlin, and even more when Mrs. Saunders had arrived at her door, heavy with her second.

But knowledge wasn't the same as knowing.

Warmth pooled, drifting down and settling between her legs as Jenny looked up at Moses. Her arm had slipped through his without any thought, and his proximity sustained her on the slow walk back. It had been a long day.

"You're staring at me," said Moses conversationally.

Jenny blanched. "No, I'm not."

She was. But he didn't need to know that.

He was a duke. A duke! Dukes did not accompany doctors of any type around a village, delivering food parcels for those without and checking on scrapes and cuts, let alone chopping wood for old ladies.

They did not look like this, either. Nearly all the dukes Jenny had seen were gruff old men with whiskers. Not . . . not . . .

"You're still staring at me."

"Staring is a very strong word," said Jenny, forcing her attention to the path ahead. "I was looking."

"And what were you looking at, precisely?"

She grinned, dipping her head in embarrassment. "You."

Moses's laugh made the warmth between her legs quicken. *Oh, hell, she knew what that was supposed to mean.*

"Well, that's honest, I suppose," he said ruefully. "And what do you see?"

Jenny welcomed the excuse to look at him again. A handsome man, she could say. A kind man. A gentle one, despite your strength. A man who surely should not be content spending day after day with her, an irritable woman who likes her own company better than any other.

Almost any other.

"I see a duke," Jenny said softly. The lane was empty, and they could speak openly here. "A duke who did not have to leave his life of luxury and serve his country, but who did."

Moses rolled his eyes. "You make that sound far more noble than it actually was. I was bored, remember?"

"A duke who served as a spy, yet seems happy to while away his days pottering about in my workroom and arguing with me,"

Jenny continued. She'd begun, she may as well finish. "And I can't help . . . I can't help but wonder . . ."

Words failed her.

Which was no great surprise. How could one capture the strange sense that she had known him forever? Her whole life. Even though she knew full well Moses had only stepped into her life—well, been dragged, truth be told—a few weeks ago.

Had this ever happened before? *Perhaps there was a malady that explained this*, Jenny thought feverishly as they turned a corner and a pair of wood pigeons flew out of the hedgerow.

Something other than love.

"Wonder what?" Moses prompted her softly.

Jenny hesitated. But there did not appear to be anything she could not say to this man. She had never felt more comfortable around anyone, which was impossible to explain.

Why not tell him the truth?

Some of it, anyway.

"You said. The other day," Jenny began awkwardly. *Why was her heart thumping so painfully?* "That you were impressed by me."

"I think I said you were impressive, actually," said Moses briskly. "And I stand by it. You are a formidable woman, Jenny Powell."

She winced. "You make me sound like an Amazon."

"Yes, I suppose I do. I suppose you are, in a way," he said with a squeeze of her arm that left her breathless. "You certainly have more fire in you than I would have expected any woman to have who was born without rank and privilege."

He could not have guessed. No one had, in all the time she had been living in East Langdon. She had given them no cause to be suspicious. Had she, finally, been found out?

"And as you are just—well, not *just a woman*—that makes it sound awful—"

"You are one of the most incredible men I have ever met," Jenny said in a rush.

Moses halted.

His lack of movement was so sudden, and her arm was so tightly encased in his own, she had no choice but to stop with him. But she swung around a bit as her momentum carried forward, so that Jenny's chest ended up—somehow—pressed up against his own.

Jenny swallowed, and the movement seemed to drag Moses's gaze down to her throat before it returned, by way of her lips, to her eyes.

"I . . . I am?" he said quietly.

She nodded. She had to tell him . . . something—she hardly knew what—but she knew she had to say it, even if she would regret it.

He had humbled himself, had he not? Moses had apologized, which was more than she had ever expected from the argumentative duke. At least, not from the argumentative man who had arrived. Moses had softened, though how she could not tell. But she needed to tell him.

"You are so kind," Jenny said quietly in the softness of the crisp silence. "Kindness in a man is so underappreciated, and you—you do not consider yourself too important to be so."

"No, I suppose not," Moses said softly, lifting a hand, tracing her jaw from ear to chin.

The subtle movement was nothing—at least, it would have been nothing if performed by another.

But having Moses's hand on her, his finger delicately caressing her . . . it made Jenny feel sensations she had never experienced. And a desire was building in her, a need to be closer. But how much closer could she possibly be?

"I didn't like you, when you first came round from your fever—"

"I thought you were complimenting me!"

Jenny laughed. "I am, I suppose. I just mean, I had presuppositions about you that were entirely wrong, I can see that now. Every moment I spend with you, I . . . I like you more."

This was a mistake. She had promised herself she would not

get involved with any man—it would distract her from being a doctor. From serving the people of East Langdon.

But Moses wasn't just a man. He was the only man who had ever made her feel like this. As though every inch of her was tingling in anticipation of something she did not know. As though this ache was both welcome and desperately needing to be satisfied. As though his kiss was the only thing that could cure her.

Jenny licked her lips and tried not to whimper as she saw the flash of desire in Moses's eyes.

He wanted to kiss her. And she certainly wanted him to kiss her.

But it was up to her to say something. Moses was too much of a gentleman to—

"If you had not exacted a certain promise from me," said Moses in such a low voice it was almost a growl, "I would be kissing you right now."

Somehow his other hand had caught around her waist. Where the basket was, Jenny did not know. She did not care.

All that she cared about was Moses.

"Kiss me."

His lips captured hers before she could finish the words. Jenny moaned, clasping her hands around his neck and pulling him closer. Deeper, that's what she wanted from this kiss—and though she could not explain it in words, she could certainly do so in the only manner of communication left to her.

With her body.

Moses's tongue was teasing along her lips, causing bliss to cascade through her. Longing overwhelmed Jenny as she opened her mouth and welcomed him in.

He seemed to know precisely what to do. Tilting her head and cradling it with a hand, Moses's tongue darted into her mouth, causing a sensual explosion to spark between her legs.

"Jenny," he moaned into her mouth.

Stars were bursting in the corners of Jenny's vision, but she did not care. She wanted this, him, all of—

Footsteps. Footsteps, in the lane.

As suddenly as the kiss had begun, it ended. Moses swiftly reached down and picked up the abandoned basket and Jenny had barely gained her balance, head spinning, when he took her arm.

"Walk," he hissed.

"What?" Jenny asked, hardly able to take it in. She had been kissing him, and now she was not. Why wasn't she?

"Ah, Doctor Powell!"

Footsteps. Of course.

Jenny beamed at the approaching vicar, a greatcoat wrapped tightly around him. "Reverend!"

"Miss Powell, what a delight to see you—and just in time, too!" The vicar smiled as he put out his hands. "My poor fingers—I need more of your ointment! I was wondering . . ."

Moses tightened his grip on her arm and Jenny fought the instinct to push aside the vicar and hasten back to her cottage with the handsome man beside her.

She could not lose her head. Kissing Moses—yes, it was rather pleasant. Very pleasant, actually.

But she could not—would not—allow herself to risk everything she had built. A duke with that much experience in kissing?

She'd never survive him.

CHAPTER THIRTEEN

5 October 1811

THE NIGHT HAD fallen faster than Moses had expected.

"Don't get rained on!" Jenny called out from the cottage.

A smile slipped across his face just to hear her voice as the sunset shot long shadows across the lawn.

"I'm almost finished!" Moses called back, placing the second to last log on the tree stump and weighing the ax in his hands.

Just over a month ago, he could never have expected his shoulder would heal so well. The knife wound—the stab wound, really—had been so close to his shoulder blade, Moses had thought there would never be the same movement, the same flexibility, the same strength.

And yet here he was, chopping wood.

Moses flexed his fingers around the handle of the ax as he lifted it up above his head. The weight of the implement shifted down through his wrist, his elbow, into his shoulder . . .

And there was no pain.

He swung the heavy ax, exulting in the swing, the power, the sense of urgency.

Thock!

The two halves of the log fell down either side of the tree stump as a little smattering of rain started to fall.

"Moses?"

A flicker of warmth shot through him. When had this happened? This routine, this sense of home he and Jenny had somehow built together—when had it been created? When had this place, this rambling cottage in the middle of nowhere, started to feel more like home than any other place he had lived? No manor, no mansion, no great hall or even palace had ever felt quite so welcoming as this.

Jenny had stuck her head out of a window. "It's raining!"

"Just one more log," Moses called back, glancing at the pile beside him—at what had been a pile near an hour ago, but was now one solitary log.

"You'll get soaked!"

"I'm almost finished!"

She was right, though Moses was hardly about to admit it. As he picked up the last log, the rain started coming down heavier. His fingers slipped just half an inch on the ax handle as he lifted it up for the last time for that evening.

It was satisfying to see the log split into two. The trouble was, Moses saw it through raindrops now dripping down his forehead.

"Damn it," he muttered with comfortable ease as he picked up the two halves and popped them in the log store against the side of the house.

He hadn't bothered to wear the jacket. Cutting up logs was a hot business, something else he had learned while living with Jenny. He'd never done such a thing while living as the Duke of Chetnole. He had people for that. His people probably had people for that.

Which meant he had never experienced the joy of physical labor performed for the betterment of another. Oh, boxing, riding, hunting, even fighting for one's life and clambering up trees to avoid French soldiers—he had experienced those labors, to be sure. But not this. Not feeling the strain and tug in one's shoulders in the service not of oneself, but of someone who . . . who mattered more.

What else, Moses wondered as he tucked the ax behind the logs where it belonged, and half walked, half ran to the back door, *had he missed?*

"You are absolutely soaked!" cried Jenny as he stepped into the workroom.

Moses grinned, pushing back his wet hair with a damp hand. "Only a tad."

"Only a—Moses Warwick, I can see through your shirt!"

Now that was interesting. Jenny appeared horrified she had made that particular comment, placing her hands over her mouth in astonishment, cheeks red.

Then she turned away and looked at the cooking pot on the fire she was tending. "You . . . you'll have to change. You'll catch a chill, staying in those wet clothes."

Moses stood dripping in the doorway and hesitated.

Well, it wasn't like Jenny hadn't seen him without his shirt. When he had been lost in the feverish dreams that had kept him asleep those first days, she had tended to his wound, cleaned it, applied her medicines to it. *It was just a body*, he tried to convince himself. Everyone had one. There was no need to be funny about it.

Still. There was something different between a senseless man being cared for by a doctor and a healthy man taking off his shirt before a lady.

But Jenny had made no motion to step out of the room or instruct him to go into the corridor and change there. Quite the contrary. Moses watched as her attention flicked momentarily to him before returning to the fire.

A slow smile crept across his face. By God, she wanted him to strip off here where she could see him, didn't she?

"Kiss me."

Moses had tried, as best he could, not to think about the kiss they had shared in the lane. She had asked him, and he had obeyed immediately, relieved Jenny had finally spoken the desire he had presumed was deep within her.

But now there was a strange awkwardness between them. Neither had spoken of it, and as far as he could see, neither would.

Perhaps this would shift the conversation forward . . .

Without even bothering to undo his buttons, Moses lifted his shirt over his head and removed the sodden linen from his body. His muscles flexed, his shoulder twisting over his head. Then he stood there, wet shirt in one hand.

He was not imagining it. Jenny was looking at him.

Oh, surreptitiously, of course. A casual observer may not notice she was doing it. But Moses knew Jenny's ways, knew the way she typically focused on the fire when she was cooking. He saw the way her eyes darted over to him, taking in every inch of his now revealed torso.

"Y-You're all wet," Jenny stammered.

Moses glanced at his chest. Yes, water droplets trickled down, meandering along the ridges of his muscles, clinging to the wiry hairs growing thicker the farther down he looked.

"Yes," he said quietly. "Yes, I suppose I am."

A thrill of expectation poured through him. There was something happening here, something he did not fully understand but wanted to rush into.

But Jenny was not the sort of woman you could rush.

"Let me get you a—"

"A towel is all I—"

They looked at each other, Jenny now straightened up with flushed cheeks.

Moses saw it all with satisfaction. "Did you say something about a towel?"

"Y-Yes, there's one over here," she said, averting her eyes as she crossed the room, as though he were a temptation too great to look at.

Oh God, that she might give into temptation . . .

Moses stepped forward, hand outstretched, as Jenny pulled a towel from a dresser drawer. "Thank you—"

"Oh, I think it would be best if a professional did this," Jenny said, holding the towel close to her. "Don't you think?"

Her eyes met his. Not boldly, yet without the reticence he would have expected from a lady in the presence of a man who was half naked.

But remember, Moses tried to remind himself. *She's a doctor. She sees men in this state all the . . . Christ. All the time.*

"A professional?" he repeated, trying to buy time. What on earth could she mean?

Jenny made it quite clear what she meant with her next movements. She stepped toward him, lifting the towel delicately, then circled him and gently patted his previously injured shoulder with the towel.

Moses quivered. Dear God, was there anything more intimate than this? What, was he supposed to just stand here and let the woman dab him dry while she got a closer look at him?

A nerve in his temple jumped. *How would he have the self-control not to sweep her into his arms and—*

"Yes, a medical professional should ensure you don't catch a cold," came Jenny's quiet voice beside him as the towel was once again pressed against his back. "I would hate for you to receive subpar care under my watch."

Moses did everything he could not to sigh as Jenny delicately pressed the towel into the small of his back, just above his buttocks. Did she have any idea what she was doing to him? How impossible it was to keep his hands to himself forever?

"I wouldn't like to argue with a professional," he croaked.

Jenny's light chuckle shot longing through him like an arrow.

Moses closed his eyes, just for a moment, then opened them again. He couldn't take much more of this—but he had to.

He was a gentleman and Jenny was a lady. An unprotected lady. With no father, no brother, her reputation was all she had. The villagers of East Langdon would certainly not accept the ministrations of a doctor who was also a fallen woman.

No, as great a temptation as Jenny was, he couldn't—

"Your shoulder has healed up nicely," Jenny said softly as she came around him, gently drying off his shoulder blade and upper arm.

Every graze of the fabric sparked desire in Moses that was growing to an ache that could not be fulfilled. It was cruelty, really, but he could not stop her.

Oh God, that she never stopped . . .

"It's thanks to you that the shoulder is as good as new," Moses murmured as Jenny moved to stand before him, her deft fingers moving the towel over his chest. If this carried on much longer, she'd be able to see the physical effect it was having on his—

"I'm glad to have been of service," Jenny said, looking at his chest as she dried off the last droplets of rain. "Being a doctor is all I ever wanted. Until . . . until recently, that is."

Moses swallowed.

Hell's bells, he was in trouble now. It was clear what she wanted, even if Jenny could not fully articulate it herself.

They had grown too close. It was a trap of their own making, a sense of togetherness that had come about because he had chosen to stay and she had chosen to open her life to him.

But now, Moses could see, there was only one direction this connection could go. And with such attraction between them, almost buzzing audibly in the air, how could he deny what he wanted?

Jenny. All of her.

"Well, I wouldn't want you to give up being a doctor, just because things might have . . . might be changing."

Jenny's bright eyes met his. "Why not?"

"Why not?" *Did the sun ever ask why it should keep shining?* "Because you are—Jenny, you must know you are the best doctor I have ever encountered."

Her eyes widened and she stepped back, towel falling to her

side. Somehow, and Moses cursed himself for having done it, he had broken the moment between them.

And most importantly, Jenny was no longer touching him. *Damn.*

"The best doctor?" she repeated uncertainly.

Moses nodded. *Should he put a shirt on? Damn it, he had no idea.* "I've encountered quite a few in my time, and—"

"The best doctor that you've ever encountered?" Jenny said again, a frown creasing her forehead.

It was strange—somehow the compliment had raised a barrier between them. The throbbing ache of desire hadn't left Moses's chest, nor lower down, but apparently it had ended any interest in her.

Moses pulled a hand through his hair and tried not to think about what he had begun to presume he would be enjoying that evening. *That is what happens, my boy, when you get ahead of yourself . . .*

"You can't mean that."

He shrugged as Jenny took another step back. "I wouldn't say it if I didn't mean it."

"But you must have met many doctors," she said slowly.

It was not a number he had ever thought to keep count of. "Probably . . . oh, a dozen. Even the famed Doctor Walsingham who has become so popular with the nobility, though I don't see—"

"I have heard of him," Jenny said.

Moses frowned. "How?"

It was not perhaps the most elegant of questions, but it was worth asking. Here Jenny was, in the middle of the Kentish countryside, with no friends or family to speak of. Surely the popular Doctor Walsingham had never drifted this far from London? It was his understanding the man never went anywhere else unless expressly sent for. With coin.

It appeared, however, that despite the simplicity of his question, the answer was not so simple.

Jenny's color had risen again, and she was twisting the towel in her hands. "I . . . my brother sometimes . . . he has been mentioned to me."

Now that was curious. Moses took a step toward her. "Your brother?"

Had she ever mentioned a brother before? Though he wracked his brains, Moses could not recall any mention of any siblings. A father, yes. A mother must presumably have existed at one point or another. But a brother?

"I did not realize you had a brother."

Jenny shrugged—or at least, gave that sort of shrug a person gives when they wish to appear nonchalant and easy. Moses could spot it from a mile off. Any spy could.

"And you are in contact with him?" A brother complicated matters. Moses was no rogue—he would have made love to Jenny willingly if she had asked for it, offered herself. But with a brother looming in the background . . .

Yet she was shaking her head. "I have not heard from him for three years—nor my mother. They . . . well, after the death of my father, I was determined to be a doctor."

Moses nodded. Yes, he had already heard this part of the story.

"My mother . . . she was . . . she thought my place . . ."

Ah. Well, he should have expected that. He had been mightily surprised to find a doctor who was a woman, after all. What mother of a daughter with no prospect other than matrimony, particularly after the death of the father, would wish for her child to hope for something so ridiculous?

Mrs. Powell could not have known what her daughter would become.

"She did not think I could succeed," said Jenny finally, lifting her chin with the defiance he had grown to know and love.

Wait—love?

"But you have," pointed out Moses quietly.

Jenny's expression was pained. "She doesn't know. I swore,

when I left that house, that they—my mother and brother—would have to write for my forgiveness before I would ever deign to write to them."

He could well imagine it. "And they have not?"

"My brother wrote once, while I was in Berlin. He advised me to seek out a Doctor Walsingham when I returned to England. He was apparently of great repute, and my brother wished me to . . . to act as his nurse."

Moses winced. Even never having met the brother, he could predict just how Jenny would feel toward that suggestion. "Ah."

"I did not reply," said Jenny stiffly, though a wry smile did appear to be lilting her lips. "And that was the last I heard of them."

Moses sighed. It must be difficult when there was no nobility, nor title, nor familial wealth to keep a family going. With Mr. Powell dead, and presumably Jenny's brother inheriting whatever trade the Powells were in, there would have been pressure upon Jenny to marry well and remove herself from the family home. The family finances.

An expensive trip to Germany for finishing school might have been the last of the family's wealth. And what had she done with it? Slipped into a university and watched surgeons cut up cadavers.

"I don't imagine your brother is that pleased with you," Moses said with a dry laugh.

There was a glint in Jenny's eye as she replied. "No. No, the Earl of Armstrong has been most displeased with me ever since."

Moses stared.

He must have heard wrong. Perhaps he had some water in his ears. Perhaps he had accidentally hit himself on the head with the ax, and this was all some sort of fever dream.

Because he couldn't have heard what he thought he'd heard, could he?

"I am sorry, I think I misheard you," Moses said weakly to the smiling Jenny. "Could . . . could you repeat that for me?"

"I said my brother, the Earl of Armstrong, is not pleased with me," said Jenny innocently, as though what she had said was the most natural thing in the world. "Which part of that is tripping you up?"

Moses's jaw dropped. "But—but—your father then, he was the—"

"The twelfth Earl of Armstrong," nodded Jenny. "Making my brother the thirteenth. Unlucky thirteen, he always used to say when we were children. You look confused, Your Grace."

Confused did not quite cover it. Moses was reeling, the information startling him down to his very soul.

She was nobility. Jenny Powell was not merely a woman who had managed to find herself in East Langdon, Kent, as a doctor. She was a lady. Not just a lady—a Lady!

"How do you think I have lived all these years, alone in this cottage, with the villagers of East Langdon unable to pay me more than a few pence for even the most expensive of medicines?" she whispered. "I . . . well, I had rather thought you'd guessed, even if you did not know the details."

Moses shook his head slowly. "You give me too much credit, Jenny. Hang it all, that can't be your actual name, can it?"

Jenny shook her head. "I mean, not technically."

There was a dancing smile across her lips and Moses did not know what to make of it. What to make of her. "Not technically?"

She stepped toward him, closing the gap between them so quickly, Moses almost reached out for her hand.

"No, I'm not Jenny Powell. Not really," she said quietly. "I am Lady Genevieve Cotton-Powell."

Lady Genevieve Cotton-Powell. Moses stared, almost unable to take it in.

The woman who had found him injured on the Kentish moors. Who had dragged him to safety, tended his wounds, bathed him, and bound him together. Who had fed him, kept him, tolerated him, slapped him for a kiss. The woman who cared for the villagers of East Langdon without expecting a bean in return, all under a name which gave her no prestige, no respect, no honor . . .

Lady Genevieve Cotton-Powell. Jenny Powell.

She was flushing. "I don't like to use the title. Not here."

"No, I can see that," said Moses softly, lifting a hand to her cheek.

He couldn't stop himself, not now. She had revealed herself to him in a way he could not have expected, been vulnerable with him, been open. And she leaned into his touch, eyelashes fluttering, which told Moses all he needed to know.

She wanted this.

"I never wanted anyone to look at me and just see the title," Jenny said, placing her hands on Moses's bare chest. Her fingertips branded him, heat flowing through her fingers. "I wanted to serve."

"I think we have that in common," Moses said in a half-strangled voice. Pull it together, man!

"I think we have a great number of things in common," Jenny said softly, a blush in her cheeks. "Including . . . including what we want to happen next."

CHAPTER FOURTEEN

"I NEVER WANTED anyone to look at me and just see the title." Jenny knew she shouldn't be saying this, knew what it would lead to. But she couldn't fight these instincts any longer. She had to see what it felt like to have her hands on—

She almost sighed as she touched Moses. *Oh, he felt wonderful.* Somehow this was completely different to when she had tended him as a patient. Then, she had felt nothing when her fingertips brushed across the hard ridges of his stomach, but now?

Oh, this was dangerous. She was stepping down a path toward something she should not want, yet her body ached for.

Jenny swallowed. *She had to concentrate on her patients.* "I wanted to serve."

There was a moment of silence between them, save for the throbbing of her pulse in her ears. And then—

"I think we have that in common," Moses said in a half-strangled voice.

Did he feel it? Did he sense the desire burgeoning within her—that had been growing, if Jenny admitted it to herself, for weeks now?

Ever since the man had opened his eyes to what and who she was?

"I think we have a great number of things in common," Jenny

said softly, trying to ignore the heat growing in her cheeks. She should stop, she shouldn't—"Including . . . including what we want to happen next."

She almost couldn't bring herself to meet Moses's gaze, but now she had spoken those words, she knew she had to.

She wanted him. Not just because he was handsome, though Jenny could hardly argue he wasn't.

Not just because Moses was kind, though he was, even if he wasn't particularly good at showing it. Like most men, he seemed to think it was better to be strong than gentle.

But really it was because he had seen in himself something that had to change. He couldn't just be a duke forever—he had felt the call of service, and unlike so many from their background, he had actually heeded the call.

And he cared for her. Jenny could not put it into words, but she had seen it in him time and time again. The way he watched her. The way he made her feel—beautiful and clever and wanted.

Oh, so wanted.

"We shouldn't," Moses breathed, his hand still cupping her cheek.

Jenny nodded. Oh, they shouldn't. But how could they help themselves? When there was such closeness to be enjoyed, why should they deny themselves?

"I know," she said quietly. "But . . . but you're a heady man to have around, Moses. I can't—when you're here, I can't think straight."

She felt as well as heard his chuckle. "Then perhaps I should leave—"

"No!"

Moses groaned at her swift response, his free hand curling around her waist, pulling her tighter into his embrace. "Jenny . . ."

He lowered his forehead so it touched hers, and Jenny's eyelashes fluttered closed.

There was something so intimate about this moment. Not just that the man still had no shirt on—Jenny would hardly complain at that, but that wasn't the closeness she was sensing.

She had told him her true name, and he had not censured her or critiqued her for leaving her privileged life behind. And he had let slip his frustrations, his fear he would never retrieve his memory, that whatever he had been doing on that fateful night when she had found him, he would never complete.

And he was here. Moses Warwick, despite having every incentive to return to luxury and finery and his service . . . he had stayed with her.

"You are so beautiful, Jenny," Moses whispered.

Jenny's eyes snapped open. "Really?"

He looked as surprised as she felt. "No one has ever told you? You don't see yourself and recognize the beauty?"

Embarrassment twisted around her and Jenny laughed dryly as she said, "I don't even own a looking glass, Moses. Why would I waste time looking at myself?"

He pulled away at her words and she almost cried out at the lack of him. Just a minute—that was all the connection they had shared—and already she was desperate to return to it. To return to him.

Moses was frowning. *Frowning, at her!* "You honestly don't know how beautiful you are?"

Try as she might, Jenny could not prevent the humiliation from seeping into her lungs, making every breath discomforting. "Moses, you can't say—"

"I will say it because it is true," said Moses quietly. "These lips, so kissable, so sweet . . ."

Jenny tried not to whimper as Moses brushed his fingertips over her lips. The movement was slight, just a heartbeat away from a breeze, yet she wished to capture those fingers and hold them there, kiss them, worship them—

"This neck," Moses exhaled. "So elegant. So regal."

She had known, somehow, what he was going to do the moment he moved—and she did not step away. Instead, Jenny's eyes closed as Moses swept his lips just under her ear, then trailed kisses down to her collarbone.

Oh, this man knew how to woo. He knew how to make a woman feel important, feel special . . .

"These breasts," Moses growled, a guttural noise in him Jenny had never heard before. "Just . . . just perfect . . ."

As his voice trailed away, Jenny tipped back her head as his lips moved to caress her décolletage, light butterfly kisses sweeping across her chest.

The desire she thought could not be contained was spilling out through her body. Jenny did not attempt to restrain herself as her hands crept onto his broad shoulders, the scar from his wound puckered under her fingertips.

She clung to him as Moses's kisses grew in fervor, dipping lower and lower until his lips met the hem of gown's bodice. Oh, if only it were gone and Moses's kisses could have continued descending . . .

"Everything about you is beautiful, Jenny," Moses said, lifting his head to capture her lips, just for a moment, in a brief ecstasy of pleasure. "But your body is nothing to your mind, your character. God, I would worship the ground you walked on, if you'd let me."

"I would let you," moaned Jenny, lifting her lips for another kiss.

He crushed his mouth on hers, and it was like heaven and hell all tangled in one. Heavenly sensations were soaring through her, tingling through her body—yet it was hell to feel this ache growing within her, balling between her legs, and know nothing could be done about it.

Because they couldn't actually complete this dance, could they? Though Jenny almost lost herself in the hedonistic delight of Moses's wild kisses, a small part of her knew this could not end as she might wish.

With lovemaking.

He was a duke. He had a reputation to uphold, and now she had made the mistake of revealing her true name, her true standing in Society, even if she had left it behind . . . well. Moses Warwick, Duke of Chetnole, may be a spy, he may know danger—but he wasn't so foolish as to bed an earl's sister.

"Jenny," growled Moses, his hands moving to her waist, her buttocks, cupping her to his—

His manhood. Jenny gasped in his mouth and he deepened the kiss, plumbing the very depths of her mouth for all the pleasure they could share as his hard manhood pressed against her hip.

Oh, he wanted her. Somehow that knowledge heightened her own need, made her revel in the effect she was having on him. And his fingers were scrabbling against her skirts, pulling them upward, and—

Jenny gasped. "Moses?"

He was gone.

Oh, not gone. No one could have left the workroom with such speed. But he was gone from her: his hands no longer cradling her buttocks, his bare chest no longer warming her own, his devilish tongue no longer claiming hers.

Jenny blinked as though dazed. "M-Moses?"

He was standing just a few feet away and there was a look of pain on his face.

She stepped forward. "What's wrong—"

"Don't—don't tempt me," Moses said, putting up his hands as though defending himself.

Jenny halted, utterly bewildered.

True, she had never kissed another man. She had no clue what she was doing, and there was the possibility she was truly bad at it. But that was no reason for him to physically push her away . . . was it?

She swallowed. "I-I quite understand—"

"No, I don't think you do," said Moses with a rueful laugh. "Damn it to heaven and back, Jenny, but you could mold me like clay if you kissed me much longer."

Jenny stared. "Oh."

Well, that was rather a surprise. Here she was, thinking she was being swept along by her own desire, but apparently Moses's was just as strong.

So why was he standing over there, when he could be wrapped around her, kissing her?

"We shouldn't."

Jenny's face fell. *They shouldn't?*

Of course they shouldn't. Had she not been thinking just the same? Was it not ridiculous to even attempt this sort of thing without some sort of scandal finding them later?

And the villagers, a quiet part of her reminded herself. *If you lose your standing with them . . .*

"I won't ruin your innocence, Jenny," Moses said heavily. "Trust me, I'd like to—but you left behind a life of luxury for this, you sacrificed everything. I won't risk—"

"Why don't you let me be the judge of what I am willing to risk?" Jenny said, more boldly than she felt.

But the sentiment was true, from deep within her. She had always been the one to decide her own fate, even if that meant stepping away from her life and making a new one.

Moses was blinking, as though dazed. "I beg your pardon?"

"If your concern is that there will be . . . well, evidence afterward," Jenny said, flushing slightly at the euphemism for falling with child. "I can stop that."

Moses stared. "You can stop . . . you can?"

It was difficult not to laugh. He surely knew of them, did he not? Even if he had never used one, it seemed impossible that the Duke of Chetnole could have spent so much time in France and never heard of them.

Hating that every step would take her farther away, Jenny turned and walked over to one of her cupboards. She was certain she had put one in here a few months ago . . .

"Here," she said, turning and holding out an envelope.

Moses breathed a laugh. "That isn't what I think it is."

"If you think it is a French letter, then it is precisely what you think it is," said Jenny.

Well, why should she be shy? She was a doctor, after all. She knew all about the theory of this side of things, even if she'd never bothered with the practice.

"You . . . you are sure about this?" Moses said hesitantly.

She had hardly been sure of this in herself until now, but as she stood there, desperately desiring him, she knew the words had to be said. Because they were true.

"I-I have grown accustomed to having you around," she said stiffly.

For a moment, Moses just stared. Then a smile slipped across his face and he walked toward her. "Did you just say 'I love you' without saying the actual words?" he teased.

Heat scalded Jenny's face. "You know what I meant."

"But it isn't what you said," Moses pointed out, suddenly grasping her hips and pulling them forward to meet his.

Jenny gasped. She hadn't moved away from the cupboard and now Moses was pinning her against it, French letter still in her hand and the words she had most clearly said between them.

Was he not going to return them?

"You love me," said Moses quietly.

Jenny forced herself to meet his eye. She did love him—and the most striking evidence of that was that she could tolerate his presence for more than an hour. Did he still not understand how rare that was?

"Yes," she exhaled.

This kiss was just as passionate as the others, but not as hurried. It was reverent, adoring, and it melted something in Jenny she had not even realized was there.

The kiss finally ended. "And you love me."

"I don't think I said that," murmured Moses.

"I think you did. Come on."

Though she had kept this part of her life entirely separate from Moses, Jenny knew it was time for him to step into the most private part of her world.

His eyes widened as she took him by the hand and started leading him to the door. "You don't want to go outside, surely—Jenny, I want to—"

"We're not going outside."

His hand was soft in hers. Was that his pulse throbbing, faster and faster, or her own?

"Then where are we—"

"My bedchamber," Jenny said as they stepped into the corridor and she put a foot on the first step of the staircase. "Where else?"

She could see in his face as they reached the landing that Moses understood just what a momentous thing this was. No one had ever come upstairs in her cottage. It was her space, hers alone. No one had gained such an intimacy with her.

Now, no one else ever would.

"Thank you," murmured Moses as Jenny pushed open the door.

"For what?"

"For letting me in."

It was not a large bedchamber. Jenny had never needed much space as she spent almost all her waking hours in the workroom. It was therefore the simplest and cheapest arrangement that she could manage and still call the space a bedchamber.

A large bed. A trunk for her clothes. And that was all.

"It's not much," Jenny said awkwardly, closing the door behind them as she was visited by visions of what Moses was probably accustomed to.

She could well remember the bedchamber her parents had shared. Gold and paintings and ornaments and finery. A ducal bedchamber must be at least twice as impressive. And this—

"It's you," said Moses simply. "That's all I want."

How she managed to find herself once more in the man's arms, Jenny did not know. It did not matter. Once again his hands were on her buttocks, but once again they did not remain there for long.

A moan of desperation escaped her lips. "Moses—"

"I know," he said, his voice low, eager, hungry. "Just let me—there!"

Jenny gasped as her gown slipped to the floor. Somehow, his clever fingers had managed to find the ties and undo them in short order.

She saw the lust grow in Moses's eyes as he beheld her in nothing but underclothes, and she knew precisely what she could do to drive him wild.

"Take off your breeches," Jenny ordered as her hands moved to unfasten her stays.

Moses swallowed. "Take off my—"

"Now," she said teasingly, her stays falling to the floor and chemise pulled over her head.

She was naked now. Strange. Jenny had rather expected to feel discomforted the first time she shared this with a gentleman, but it felt so right, so obvious that it was him.

Moses almost fell over trying to pull off his boots and take off his breeches at the same time. "God, you are—"

"And so are you," Jenny breathed, taking all of him in.

She had been fortunate, in the three years since she had arrived in East Langdon, that no man of the area had ever suffered an injury to . . . to that. Or near there. And so this, perhaps unbeknownst to Moses, was the first time she had seen . . .

"You are magnificent," she said in wonder.

And he was. Moses's height, his breadth, his strength were all the more impressive now that he was without clothes. The way his muscles rippled with each small movement, the way his manhood stood to attention for her . . .

"I do love you, you know," said Jenny shyly, reaching out for his hands. "Even if I'm not good at saying it."

"You are not good at saying it, and I love that about you," said Moses with a laugh, pulling her close. "And now—"

"Moses!" Jenny shrieked.

It was impossible not to. Holding onto her tightly, he had

allowed them both to fall onto her bed, legs tangled, fingers grasping each other, and Jenny had never known anything so sensual, so erotic.

Somehow Moses had nestled himself between her legs, his kisses trailing down to her breasts as she had so wanted downstairs, and Jenny arched her back as peaks of pleasure threatened to rip her very limbs apart.

"I want—I want—"

"I know," Moses said, though how he could, Jenny had no idea. She could barely articulate the flurried desires cascading through her mind, instincts taking over. "Where is it?"

Jenny blinked. *Well, really.* She was the doctor, but she had presumed a gentleman would know precisely where her secret place—

"The French letter," panted Moses, appearing to strain against his desire to sink himself into her. "Where is it?"

And perhaps if she had thought for more than a moment, she might have said something different. But she didn't.

"Love me," Jenny said, clutching his shoulders and shifting her hips to try to draw him in. "Love me now, Moses."

Whether it was the way she ordered it, or the movement of her body, or just the desires that had been repressed too long, Jenny did not know.

All she knew was that she was being filled, slowly but surely, by the throbbing member of the man she adored. And by God, it felt good.

Moses groaned. "Sweet heaven, Jenny!"

Jenny could not speak. There was such tingling of decadent desire sweeping through her, she could barely think.

"I've wanted this for so long," Moses moaned, thrusting into her slowly, building a rhythm that was teasing the ache between her legs. "So long—"

"It's a perfectly natural desire for a gentleman to have," Jenny said, mind whirling.

His chuckle could be felt within her. "What, wanting to make love to you?"

"No!" *Dear God, did he think her a harlot?* "No, to—to be one with the person you love!"

"Oh, I want that," Moses said in a ragged voice, his breathing short as he kissed her, his thrusting pace increasing. "I want—I want—"

Jenny arched her back again, her hips bucking to meet his, so desperate was she for the release she could sense just on the edges of this passion. Any moment now—

"Moses!"

She peaked and it was like every inch of her bones, her muscles, her sinews roared with ecstasy. She was falling apart, every organ and heartbeat, and she did not care because this pleasure, this connection with Moses—

"Jenny, Jenny!"

And somehow he could feel it too, and they were falling together, falling through space as their bodies mingled and became one.

And then they were collapsing against the bed, Moses rolling off her and panting beside her, their hands somehow still entwined.

Jenny blinked up at the ceiling, trying to make the stars go away. "So that . . . that was lovemaking?"

She saw a wicked smile on the duke's face.

"That's one way to go about it, yes. But we have all night . . ."

CHAPTER FIFTEEN

7 October 1811

*I*T WAS DARK. *It was always dark in this nightmare, but as Moses hadn't had it for so long, it was rather a surprise.*

"Oh, blast," he said wearily.

Sometimes, his dreams were so real it was impossible to tell if he truly was dreaming. And sometimes, the nightmare returned and he knew he was in it, but he couldn't get out.

Shots were firing around him. Wincham had already been sent back to England injured, and it would be a miracle if all of them returned safely.

And he had to get back to England—he had discovered the traitor. He now knew who it was—the one who had been sharing details of their missions with the enemy. One of the men he had trusted with his life—a man no one would ever consider capable of betraying them.

And his associate had stabbed him in the back.

In the dream, Moses tried to reach around to his back to feel the wound. He was still in France, a battle raging around him, yet his shoulder was healed. How could that be? And why wasn't he in England? He had determined to leave that day for England, tell someone he trusted that there was a traitor in service to the Crown.

So why was he here?

"Jenny?" Moses said into the darkness.

Who was Jenny?

He was waking, and Moses knew the details of the nightmare would slip away as the dawn came. Would he remember there was a traitor to be uncovered? And who was this woman he felt such a craving to see . . .?

For the second morning in a row, Moses opened his eyes and wasn't sure where he was.

This wasn't the workroom. He couldn't see herbs hanging above him, nor could he smell the strange acid scent of one of Jenny's medicines, or hear the crackling of a newly lit fire.

And besides, his pallet bed had somehow inexplicably grown more comfortable, which didn't make a jot of sense. It was wider, too. And there was a woman in it . . .

Moses blinked, and the small bedchamber of Jenny Powell—or Lady Genevieve Cotton-Powell, as he supposed he should now think of her—came back into view. The large bed in the small room, the trunk just to the side by the window, and the door upon which was hanging a gentleman's dressing gown.

Something in his stomach lurched. Now he came to think about it, he really should ask Jenny whose that was. Then he glanced over and the disquiet in his stomach immediately settled. She was, after all, simply the best tonic in the world.

Naked and sleeping on her front, chestnut curls awash over the pillow, Jenny slept on.

Oh, how he loved her.

Moses had never expected this. He had figured that when he was, oh, another decade older, he would choose an obliging debutante from that year's Season, sire a few heirs upon her, then they would lead separate lives. That was what his father had done. That was what almost every duke did.

Though now he came to think about it, a few of his friends had spent the last few years marrying themselves off, and to entirely inappropriate partners.

But still. It was what he had assumed would happen.

He had certainly not counted on this. Not meeting a quiet,

inexplicable doctor in the middle of nowhere. Not slowly growing accustomed to a woman who struggled to be around people for more than five minutes together. Not discovering, completely by chance, a most eligible woman for him if he wished it . . .

Moses's heart skipped beat.

It was perhaps one of the only things he had not discussed with Jenny.

The future.

The last two days had been a whirlwind. A whirlwind of kisses and affection and pleasure. They had barely managed to keep their hands off each other long enough to do anything else at all. In fact, just when they had promised each other the day before that they absolutely would not permit themselves to make love again, and five minutes later in the workroom he had her lying on the kitchen table with his fingers in her, there had been a knock at the door. A patient.

It was a good thing Moses hadn't succumbed completely to temptation and ripped her gown off moments before. Now that would have been difficult to explain.

But in amongst all that, not once had he and Jenny discussed the future. What they could be to each other. What they should be to each other.

Moses sighed, placing a hand behind his head as he looked up at the ceiling. And he needed to discuss it.

Not just because she was a woman, and therefore deserved to know what he planned. Not merely because she was an earl's daughter, an earl's sister, whose brother could turn up at any moment—heaven forbid—and demand satisfaction.

But because he loved her.

And because of the letter which had been burning a hole in the pocket of his secondhand jacket since he had been handed it yesterday by a Mr. Guernsey.

"Son of Mrs. Guernsey?" Moses had asked warily, when the man had knocked on Jenny's door. "She doesn't want any more firewood chopped does she? I've . . . well, I've hurt my shoulder again."

Picking up Jenny Powell and trying to carry her up the stairs over my shoulder, Moses could have said, but didn't. He hadn't wished to tell her how greatly that romantic gesture had cost him. He was glad he had chopped so much firewood a few days before.

"Oh, no, sir," said Mr. Guernsey, thrusting a hand into his pocket. "I was in Canterbury you see, on business, and I happened to mention to a friend . . ."

His voice continued, but Moses did not hear a word.

He got the gist. Somehow, though he could not understand how, news of his presence at East Langdon had made its way to London—and that meant Snee, the magistrate he and the other dukes in the service of the Crown worked with, had heard.

And that meant Adam Seymour, Duke of Gilroyd, had heard.

Moses winced slightly as he leaned over the side of the bed and pulled at his jacket. He'd read the letter there and then, Mr. Guernsey having bowed and left him to it. The words had caused an ache which had not dissipated.

He pulled the letter from his jacket pocket and leaned back in bed to read it again. Why, he did not know. Moses had almost committed the whole thing to memory as it was.

Chetnole,

It's been an absolute devil to find you, I hope you know. When we received word you had left France, I waited at Dover for an absolute age and spent far too much on whelks, the disgusting things. By the time I assumed you hadn't made it, I sent word to London for you.

Imagine my surprise when the letter was returned by your steward. They hadn't seen you.

The newspapers got hold of the story. No matter what I try to do, they always manage to get a hold of something. It's galling in the extreme.

Still, it has helped in a way. Half the country is on the lookout for you. I'm afraid someone got hold of an engraving of that portrait of you at Chetnole Lacey, worse luck. You'll never be able to go back to France as a spy, as the whole country knows your face. I would imagine some of their spies here have memorized it. It's what I'd do.

Despite all that, it's taken weeks to find you. I'm not even sure that the mention of a tall stranger turning up in a Kentish village with an injured shoulder is you.

It sounds like the sort of bloody-minded thing you'd do, though.

I don't know why you're hiding out there so long—I presume you've tracked someone interesting down, though what they'd be doing in a place called East Langdon, I dread to think.

It's time to come back to London, Chetnole. You have information we need, information that can break through this ridiculous war and send Napoleon back where he belongs.

Bring whatever girl you found there. Shot in the dark, of course, but I can't think what else could be keeping you there.

Snee and I will be waiting in London. Don't take your time.

Gilroyd

Moses sighed heavily, then glanced quickly at Jenny. She did not stir, undisturbed by his heavy conscience.

That was the ache in his chest. The guilt. The knowledge that as soon as he was able, he should have got on the road, by hook or by crook, and made his way to London. Whether his entire memory had returned, or none of it had.

There were people depending on him and he had let them down. Were his desires for Jenny truly more important than his work in France? More important than the lives of others?

Moses's jaw tightened. True, if he had recalled precisely why he had left France for England in the first place, perhaps he would have not had the excuse to stay. If he could remember who had stabbed him in the back—and why—perhaps he would have felt the impulse to return immediately. But as it was . . .

"I'll stay up with you."

"You will?"

"Anything to spend more time with you."

Moses sighed. As it was, he had stayed. And Jenny Powell had wormed her way into his affections without him even knowing. Without her really knowing she was doing it.

And the guilt that his friends had been searching for him, concerned he was missing—that the whole of England, it appeared, now knew he had been serving as a spy in France and had suddenly disappeared . . .

It weighed on his heart.

While he had been busy falling in love and gallivanting around the workroom of a doctor in a small Kentish village, the rest of the world had continued.

And soon he would have to rejoin it.

Jenny snuffled in her sleep. Moses glanced over at her as she turned over, a teasing glimpse of her breasts hidden partially by the blanket.

How could he leave her?

"Did you just say 'I love you' without saying the actual words?"

"You know what I meant."

"But it isn't what you said."

Moses smiled, despite the concern balled up tight in his chest. How could he walk away from the greatest connection he had ever known? How could he abandon the woman he loved?

"I've wanted this for so long."

He did not have to ask whether Jenny would come with him.

Leave East Langdon? Leave her cottage and her workroom? More importantly, leave everything she had built—everything that she had worked for, against the odds, against her family's wishes, against what the world expected of her? Return to the Society she had left, the disapprobation of her family, the scandal that would erupt at her return?

Disappointment crept in to join the guilt, overshadowing the happiness Moses had felt at waking up next to this remarkable woman.

No, he didn't need to ask. He knew what the answer would be, and he couldn't bear to hear it from Jenny's own lips.

If he told her he wanted her to come back with him to London, she would decline. And he would have to leave with that memory ringing in his ears.

Jenny had built a life here. Moses could not help but admire it. He'd never built anything that had lasted more than a few weeks. His networks in France proved that.

She wouldn't sacrifice it for him—and he wouldn't ask her. Moses refused to put the woman he loved in a position like that. He wouldn't ask Jenny to tear herself in half in the questioning of it, not when he knew what she would decide in the end. He wouldn't make her choose, not when there was no shadow of a doubt in Moses's mind that she would choose doctoring over him. Over what they could have together.

He took a deep breath and glanced once more at the letter.

> *It's time to come back to London, Chetnole. You have information we need, information that can break through this ridiculous war and send Napoleon back where he belongs.*
>
> *Bring whatever girl you found there. Shot in the dark, of course, but I can't think what else could be keeping you there.*
>
> *Snee and I will be waiting in London. Don't take your time.*

They were right. They did need him. And wasn't that precisely why Moses had entered into this life of service to the Crown in the first place? To be needed?

He shifted in the bed, unable to settle.

Everything he thought he wanted was in London. Everything he knew he wanted was in East Langdon. *Damn and blast it all to—*

"Now that's a particularly dour look," said a quiet, yet teasing voice. "What on earth has happened since I last saw you to warrant such an expression?"

All the tension melted away as Moses turned to see Jenny awake. Mostly awake.

"What time is it?" Jenny asked sleepily.

"You mean, do you have to get up yet?" Moses ribbed.

It had astonished him, these last few days, that there was more to discover about Jenny Powell. He had thought he knew almost everything about her, yet there was clearly more to learn. Like, for example, that she was most definitely not a morning person.

Jenny groaned as she sank back into her pillows. "I don't want to get up, but there's a salve downstairs—"

"I'll help you," said Moses gently.

She blinked blearily. "And I've got to cut up—"

"I can do that," he said. "Badly, but I can do it."

Her smile said precisely what Jenny thought of Moses's cutting ability. "And if I said I have my rounds to do, to ensure everyone is doing well in the village, you would say—"

"I'll carry the basket, and you can hold onto my arm, and I'll be with you," said Moses, a knot tying itself in his throat. "Every step of the way."

Her swift kiss before diving back to her pillow again, hugging it happily as she allowed her eyes to close, was everything.

Never before had Moses regretted his station, his accident of birth. Being born a duke, it was a privilege. One he had been conscious of from a young age. Serving the Crown was something not everyone could do. Traveling the world, knowing he was making a difference. They were all parts of himself he had once prized.

No longer. Now all he wanted to do was be Jenny Powell's husband and for them to spend their lives here in this tiny cottage.

Moses started. *Marry Jenny? Now that was a thought he hadn't consciously had before.*

The letter had been stuffed beneath his pillow when Jenny woke, but as her eyes closed again, he slowly brought it out and read it through one more time.

Despite all that, it's taken weeks to find you. I'm not even sure the mention of a tall stranger turning up in a Kentish village with an injured shoulder is you.

It sounds like the sort of bloody-minded thing you'd do, though.

It was the sort of bloody-minded thing he would do. And it was all he could do not to write back to Gilroyd and tell him the whole thing was off, that he wanted out. He wouldn't go back to that life, not now that he'd found a new one.

What was it he had said to Jenny once in jest?

"You know what they say. A duke a day keeps the doctor away."

A wry smile curled his lips. Well, he had been partly right. This doctor was keeping this duke away from his duties, his responsibilities. And by God, he wanted to let her.

"Moses?"

Moses shoved the letter back under his pillow just as Jenny opened her eyes again, his pulse hammering. That had been a close one. Now he had read it through again, it was probably safer to burn the dratted thing rather than risk it falling into the wrong hands.

Like Jenny's, for instance . . .

"What's wrong?" Jenny asked quietly.

Moses forced himself to shrug. "Wrong? Nothing's wrong."

Nothing could be further from the truth, but he wasn't going to tell her that. He could not allow her to know just what efforts were being put into finding him. Her sense of honor, of duty, may even make her order him to return.

Moses's stomach swooped dangerously, making nausea rise. He wasn't sure how he could face that.

"You don't have to lie to me, you know," Jenny said quietly, placing a hand on his chest. "I know you."

Moses responded to the simplest of her touches. "I know."

"You can trust me with any of your worries," Jenny continued softly, as rain started to patter against the windows. "I . . . I want us to be open with each other. To share our thoughts."

To share everything.

That was what Moses wanted her to say. He wanted to forget London even existed, that Snee and Gilroyd were waiting for him, that he had any burden to bear back there with him.

He wanted to share his life with Jenny, not keep secrets or tell lies.

"Moses?"

"It's nothing," he said quickly, placing a hand over her own. "Honestly."

He had never planned to lie to Jenny. But how could he ever begin to explain, how could he even find the words? It wasn't nothing—it wasn't even something. It was everything, the heavy burden resting in him. Demanding that he do the honorable thing and leave behind the woman he loved.

"It's not nothing," said Jenny with a frown, moving from sleep to full wakefulness. "Moses—"

"It's my shoulder."

Her frown deepened, though the urgency with which she spoke dissipated. "Your shoulder?"

It was *a* truth, after all. Perhaps not the truth that Jenny had been prodding for, but the truth nonetheless.

"Yes, I think I injured it slightly yesterday when . . . well," he grinned.

Jenny stared blankly, then flushed. "Oh. Oh!"

"There'll be no more carrying you up the stairs over my shoulder again for a while," Moses said ruefully, reaching out and pulling Jenny into his arms.

The need in her roused him, as he had known it would. *Just one more day*, he promised himself. One more day with Jenny. A perfect day. Filled with laughter and love and service. With lovemaking and conversation.

One more perfect day.

"But you can still . . ."

Moses blinked. "What?"

There was a mischievous look on Jenny's face that he rarely

saw. She was always so serious—probably because, he reasoned, she had rather serious responsibilities.

"You can still make love, though, can't you?" Jenny said, her voice low as one of her hands started wending its way down his chest.

Moses groaned as parts of him started to stiffen. "You know, I don't know."

"Well," said Jenny softly, kissing the corner of his mouth as her hand finally found his manhood. "There is only one way to find out . . ."

CHAPTER SIXTEEN

8 October 1811

I T DID NOT occur to Jenny to worry when Moses was nowhere to be found that morning.

She had entered the workroom as usual to find a fire lit in each of the grates and a new stack of firewood between them, ready to feed the flames.

A smile drifted across her face. He was so thoughtful. He was always saying how much easier it would be to have the log pile inside. And he was right.

Picking up two logs and placing one on each fire, Jenny cast her gaze around the room, lighting on his makeshift bed.

Warmth suffused her chest. *Well, that would no longer be necessary.*

"Did you just say 'I love you' without saying the actual words?"

"You know what I meant."

"But it isn't what you said."

Ever since they had admitted their feelings for each other, there had been no thought of Moses remaining down here when it came to retiring for the night. There was only one place he belonged, and that was beside her in her bed upstairs. Or over her. Or, for the first time last night, beneath her.

And though they had not attempted it, Jenny could not help but feel it would be rather difficult to make love in a bed as small as that pallet. Though she wasn't averse to trying.

She shivered, the memories of their lovemaking heating her far better than the fire ever could. She could never have predicted how the arrival of that bedraggled man would affect her. How dramatically her life would change. How she would never be the same again.

The fact he was not here, right in this moment, was neither here nor there. Moses had taken to walking into the village most mornings. To stretch his legs, he said.

Jenny knew better, and she clasped her arms around her as she breathed in deeply, resplendently happy. He did it to ensure she had an hour or two to herself every day. Having Moses here was almost like being alone, she was now so comfortable with him. But not quite. He knew her better than perhaps she knew herself and saw how much she valued her time alone. Without it, she struggled to get through to the evening.

Humming a song to herself as she packed away the camp bed, Jenny could not help but feel that it was a statement about the future. Their future.

Though they had not discussed it, she was certain it could only tend to one direction: Moses staying with her in the village. Getting married by the reverend in the church by the green. Perhaps one day raising a family.

Jenny's stomach lurched and she paused after lifting the heavy bed. Not that she expected that to happen any time soon.

"Right," she said aloud to the empty workroom, luxuriating in the time to herself. "Herbs."

It was her habit on a Tuesday to run through the inventory of her cupboards and drawers and make a list of the herbs and plants she was short of. She could dry most things, but not all, and it was useful for the inhabitants of East Langdon who often traveled to larger villages and towns to know what she was on the lookout for.

Jenny spent a happy hour or so in silence, save for her own humming, running through her catalogue of salves, lotions, and potions, as Moses had once called them.

Her stomach twisted happily. He did have a way with his nonsense.

Then there were the linens to wash, which took a great deal of effort, not to mention fetching water from the well to do it. Then the table needed to be scrubbed with the best soft soap she could find, then there was that chapter she had intended to read again in *A Modern Examination of the Human Body and Its Many Complexities* . . .

In fact, it was only when her stomach started to rumble that Jenny realized how late it was in the day.

She glanced over at the small carriage clock. Two o'clock.

Jenny blinked. *Surely not. The entire morning had got away from her—she had not realized it was that late!*

And where was Moses?

The thought shot through her like a bolt of lightning, unsettling her just as the sudden weather change often did.

He had been working on improving his stamina. He had told her it was so he could keep up with her in the bedchamber, which she had laughed at.

Still. He had been gone quite a while. Though Jenny had been sleeping in longer in the mornings now that she had a helper to complete her daily tasks, he must still have been gone by—oh, half past nine or so. Surely he could not have gone rambling to the village for over four hours?

Perhaps he had been accosted by Mrs. Guernsey, she thought as her stomach rumbled again. There would be no harm in eating luncheon before he returned. And in the silence, she could read more of her book. She may as well make hay while the sun shined.

And so Jenny curled up in an armchair with a good book and one of the summer apples she had so carefully stored, and settled herself in for a little more reading.

It was only when a log slipped in the grate making her start that she looked up again.

The workroom was gloomy. Evening had come, far more swiftly than she had expected now that the days were growing shorter. She would have to build up the fire again, and—

Wait. Evening?

Jenny rose, book slipping from her hands to her lap to the floor as she stepped toward her clock on the table.

Could it have stopped? But no, that didn't make any sense. If the timepiece had stopped, it would show an earlier hour, not a later one. It said it was almost twenty past five.

She turned to the window. It was evening; the sun had gone taking with it its joy, and she was alone.

Where was Moses?

Something akin to fear encircled her heart. Was it possible— could something have happened to him? It was not like Moses to go hours and hours without her. It was not, now she came to think about it, usual for her to go hours and hours without him. His absence was like an ache, a hole scooped out that she had not realized was missing.

Jenny swallowed. *If he was hurt, if Moses had come to some sort of trouble . . .*

And the letter which he had thought himself so clever to hide resurfaced in her mind.

"What's wrong?"

"Wrong? Nothing's wrong."

Jenny bit her lip. Everyone should be allowed to have secrets, even within the loving affection they had found. She had not deemed it important enough to point out how poorly Moses had hidden the letter he had received. She had presumed that, in time, he would share its contents with her if they were in any way meaningful.

But another day had slipped by and he had not said any- thing—and now he was missing.

Moses is not missing, Jenny thought. *He's just not . . . here. Right now. As she had expected him to be.*

That was all. Missing meant panic and pain and seeking out someone who perhaps could not be found. And that was not going to be her and Moses's story. It just couldn't be.

Despite all her finer feelings, however, Jenny could not settle. Torn between remaining at the cottage to berate Moses when he returned and leaving West Cottage to go and look for him, she paced around the workroom trying to decide what to do when a knock sounded from her front door.

The tension in Jenny's shoulders immediately eased. "Finally! You know, I was really starting to worry—"

Her feet had taken her into the corridor and to the front door before her reason could catch up with her. Why would Moses knock? He knew the door was never locked and would have no reason to ask permission to come in. This was his home now.

But those thoughts had not quite fully sunk in as Jenny opened the door. "There you—oh. Mr. Guernsey."

He was standing on her doorstep with a worried look in his eyes. Jenny had seen it before. She knew it well. Her concerns about Moses would simply have to wait. When she had a patient on her doorstep—

"Miss Powell—Doctor Powell, I mean," said the man, bowing. "Erm . . ."

It was going to be one of those, Jenny thought. *An awkward one. Please, not something near his—*

"I was asked to give you this."

Jenny blinked. There was a letter in the man's hands.

A letter? For her?

Her lungs were suddenly tight with panicked anticipation. After all these years, her mother or brother must have finally decided to reach out to her. What on earth could that letter contain? More censure? More denial of who she was, what she was, what she had worked so hard to become?

Or perhaps words of contrition. Of forgiveness.

Not that she needed forgiveness, Jenny thought bitterly as she took the letter from the man and curtseyed in polite response. She had done nothing wrong. There was nothing she had done to be ashamed of.

Even permitting a duke to bed her again, and again, and again—

"He asked me to give it to you, see," said Mr. Guernsey uneasily. "And I said I would as soon as I was done at the smithy, and then the vicar came by with something to mend, and we got to talking, and you know how Vicar can be for talking . . ."

Jenny nodded, though she was not really listening. Mr. Guernsey could rival the reverend in his ability to talk on. Instead, she examined the letter.

Though she had presumed it was from her mother or brother, she could see now without even opening it that it could not be so. The paper wasn't nearly as fine as something that a Cotton-Powell would use, and there was no seal. It was just a folded piece of paper.

She would have to hope Mr. Guernsey could be trusted.

"And he said you would want to read it straightaway, so as soon as I banked up the fire at the forge—"

"He? He asked you to do this—who is he?" Jenny interrupted.

Her brother would surely have just sent something directly, and sealed. He would not have resorted to stopping off in the village and asking a stranger to hand deliver a letter.

Who on earth could this missive be from?

"Good evening, Miss—Doctor Powell," said Mr. Guernsey, beating a hasty retreat.

Jenny watched him curiously as he went along the lane, evidently in a hurry to be out of her presence.

Was this what the herbal healers of old had been forced to deal with? People who were desperate for your help in times of need, but were awkward and distrustful when they were in full health? Had they found it as irritating as she did?

"Moses?" Jenny whispered.

Perhaps he had been returning home and seen Mr. Guernsey

and not wished to answer any awkward questions. *Yes, that was it,* Jenny thought as hope rose. He would be just out of sight, and perhaps did not know that Mr. Guernsey had gone.

"Moses?"

There was no answering smile, no cocky air, no laughing explanation as to what had kept him from her arms for so long.

And instead of facing the fact that she still did not have a clue where Moses was, Jenny turned instead to the letter in her hand.

Jenny unfolded the paper and started to read. By the time her gaze reached the third line, her hand had lifted to clutch her chest.

No. No, it couldn't be.

Jenny,

I've thought the past day how I would write this letter, and though I now have the opportunity to write it, I cannot think what to say.

Every moment with you was a true blessing. I cannot conceive of a life in which I did not meet you, and I am honored to have spent so much time in your care.

Gratitude does not fully explain what I feel for you. Without you, I know I would never have regained movement in my shoulder. My health was in your hands, and you cared for it magnificently. Thank you. And I am sorry, once again, for all the times I doubted you.

I think you know why I am writing this.

I cannot stay. Duty takes me forward, and though I still cannot remember why I decided to return to England from France, the fact is that I did. I must go on to London. I must serve my country, as you serve your little slice of England.

Making you choose between the life you have now and a life of painted finery, sitting in drawing rooms discussing the weather, not using the talents and gifts you have—I would never do that to you. You would be wasted as a duchess, but you make a spectacular doctor.

I truly respect you, Jenny. I hope you will think as fondly of me as I will think of you.

I remain, as I always will, your affectionate servant—

M. W. Chetnole

Jenny stared. There was something wrong with her eyesight—that, or there was something wrong with Moses's handwriting. Large blots were appearing on the page, fuzzing the words, making them almost impossible to read.

Only when she blinked and more spoldges appeared did she realize they were being created by her tears.

He had . . . he had left her.

Jenny could hardly take it in. The pain was so sudden, so acute, that she half fell, half staggered into the door frame, still clutching the letter. How could he write such things? After all they had shared, all they had professed for each other—he could abandon her to return to his swashbuckling life as a ducal spy?

The audacity!

Making you choose between the life you have now and a life of painted finery, sitting in drawing rooms discussing the weather, not using the talents and gifts you have . . .

And so he would choose for her? He would set aside any respect he had for her, and unilaterally make the decision that would wrench them apart forever?

"Did you just say 'I love you' without saying the actual words?"

"You know what I meant."

"But it isn't what you said."

Jenny's fingers tightened on the letter as she continued to stare at it, as though that would in any way change the words on the page.

Her heart had been so full, but now it felt empty. Empty, save for the anger roaring through her, burning everything in its path, demanding she go out there and find him and—

And what?

Jenny tried to slow her breathing, which was ragged and painful. Force Moses to come back here?

She knew all too well what it was for someone to attempt to enforce their will upon another. For their vision of your life to be more important than what you actually wanted.

She could still hear her mother's words from their last meeting echoing around her mind.

"I know what is best for you, Genevieve Cotton-Powell, and I am your mother! You will obey me. You will leave behind that ridiculous idea of becoming a doctor and take up your place as a member of—Genevieve! Genevieve, come back!"

Jenny swallowed, clenching her hand with the letter from Moses still within it.

She had refused to comply to her mother's demands—but would she now so easily attempt to enforce her own desires for Moses's life on him? Was she truly that hypocritical?

The letter was cold in her fingers.

How could she have done this? Trusted a duke—an admitted spy, a man who lied for a living!

Assuming he actually was a spy.

Assuming he actually was a duke, Jenny thought with dismay. She had no reason to believe him, no evidence to support his claims. He was obviously an educated gentleman, but what did that signify?

Nothing.

Turning slowly on her feet, Jenny forced herself to return back to her workroom. The fire, fed by the logs Moses had chopped just days ago, blazed merrily as though all was right with the world.

Scalding hot tears continued to fall down Jenny's cheeks as she stood motionless in the center of the workroom, unsure what to do.

Well, a broken heart. Now that was something she had not yet treated. But even as a doctor, someone who knew the body inside out, Jenny was certain there was no quick or easy remedy for such an ailment.

She threw the letter into the fire. She watched it burn, the edges crinkling up into ashes.

"You are Doctor Powell," she said sternly. "You are a doctor. You can't just stand here as though you've got time to waste."

Striding to the table, Jenny picked up a knife and started chopping up some vegetables ready for a stew. She needed to eat. That was it. Food would make everything better.

Her tears dripped onto the chopping board, and eventually her movements slowed until Jenny was standing at the table with a knife in one hand, a potato in the other, and tears streaming down her cheeks.

It was over. He was gone.

CHAPTER SEVENTEEN

12 October 1811

STRANGE. MOSES HAD assumed that the sight of London's streets, the familiar buildings towering in the autumnal mist, the knowledge he had finally done what he had set out to do in France and returned, would have brought him joy.

If anything, it brought him quite the opposite.

Bile rose in his throat with every turn of the carriage wheels. His hands were numb, freezing from being assigned the rooftop seat.

Well . . . given. Even Moses had to admit, the driver had been most charitable by permitting him to come along at all when he had no way of paying the man until they arrived. Though Moses assumed if he did not provide the mail coach driver the promised two pounds—two whole pounds!—something rather nefarious would happen to him.

"This your house?" sneered the coach driver as they slowed to a stop. "Not likely."

Moses permitted himself a small grin. "As chance would have it, no. This is not my house."

He glanced up at the foreboding windows, all shadowed or boarded up; at the lamp not lit over the doorway; the peeling paint of the door itself.

No, he would never permit his home to fall into such disrepair. And in Mayfair, too! What were Gilroyd's servants thinking of?

"Wait here," Moses said aloud.

There was some grumbling behind him as he strode up the steps with confidence and ease. It must look strange, he supposed. A vagabond like himself—or at least, that was what he probably looked like—striding confidently up to a house which clearly belonged to a gentleman, even if that gentleman had fallen on bad times.

Gilroyd needed taking in hand, Moses could not help but think as he rang the doorbell and waited for a servant. Perhaps if he had come straight here after the tragedy, and not got so . . . so entangled in France, he might have been able to do something.

Or perhaps Gilroyd was simply determined to ruin himself.

"Oi, you, are you—"

"Give the man time to open the door," Moses said heavily, tiredness wearing his temper thin. "I just need to—ah, there we are."

The door had opened and Dawson, Gilroyd's butler, looked horrified. "Your Grace!"

"Yes, I know, I look awful," said Moses wearily. "Traveling days on the roof of a mail coach will do that. Do you have two pounds, old thing? I'll get my steward to send it along, but I need it rather urgently."

That was one of the many benefits of coming straight to Gilroyd's, Moses thought as the man's butler wordlessly handed over two one-pound notes with absolutely no questions. It made him wonder what strange requests Dawson had received from his own master over the years . . .

"Here," Moses said gruffly, stepping back to the coach and handing over the money.

The mail coach driver's eyes widened. "Hang on, you asked him for—he gave—"

"And with that, our business is concluded," said Moses with a curt nod. "Good day."

"Wait, I want to know—"

Whatever it was the man wanted to know, Moses certainly wasn't going to tell him. He wanted a bath, a large meal, and the chance to discuss weighty matters with Gilroyd. Anything to forget—

"Did you just say 'I love you' without saying the actual words?"

"You know what I meant."

"But it isn't what you said."

Hands clenched into fists that were slowly loosening, Moses stepped into the Gilroyd hallway and jerked his head. "Close that door."

It shut not with the quiet of well-oiled hinges, but with a squeaking groan that made him wince. *What on earth had Gilroyd been doing—or not doing—in this place?*

He caught the eye of the butler, who shrugged. "His Grace does not care for—"

"Who's that? I won't have any visitors," snapped an irritable voice. "What have I told you, Dawson, about opening the door to—good heavens."

A man stood in a doorway, eyes wide, mouth gaping—a tall man, with black hair, hooded eyes, and a morose expression.

Moses grinned. "Et voilà!"

Perhaps it was flippant. Gilroyd's letter *had* said, after all, that there were people looking for him, spending their time and resources to search for traces of him. But even Moses could not have expected the sudden hug his old friend gave him. Gilroyd was not a hugger.

"You absolute cretin, Chetnole, you've had us all worried half to death and here you are, fit as a fiddle!" said Gilroyd gruffly in his ear. "I don't suppose you did it on purpose, just to frighten us?"

"Nothing of the sort, old thing," said Moses with a dry laugh, clutching the man's back and wondering why this reunion did not feel as he had thought it should.

This was his life, his purpose. He was supposed to come back to London and fulfil his duty, and Gilroyd was one of his few trusted friends. So why did this all feel so . . . so empty?

"You have a great deal to explain, and I am still not sure whether I am going to forgive you," said Gilroyd menacingly as he pulled away. "But first things first."

Moses's shoulders sagged. *Yes. Food, drink, a comfortable chair—*

"You, man, need a bath," said Gilroyd, crinkling his nose. "I've got a valet here somewhere—someone may as well use him. Dawson, see to it, will you?"

It was never pleasant being informed so baldly by a friend that you stunk to high heaven, but Moses was hardly in a position to complain. It was blissful to sink into the scalding water in the ceramic bath upstairs in Gilroyd House, and Moses probably spent longer in there than he needed.

This was the moment, he told himself. *You're stepping out of a life you accidentally built in East Langdon, and back into the life you should never have left.*

You're leaving Moses behind and becoming the Duke of Chetnole once more.

It should have felt natural. So why did it fill him only with disappointment?

By the time Moses had been dressed by Gilroyd's valet and pointed in the direction of the smoking room, evening had fallen in London. There was still noise though. He had half-forgotten what it was like to live in a city after being so long with Jenny.

Jenny. He must not think her name—that was the route to madness.

"You look a damn sight better than you did, and a great deal calmer than you ought," remarked Gilroyd as Moses stepped into the smoking room. "Pull up a chair and tell me all about it."

Moses tried to smile. He really did. He tried to recall that to Gilroyd, it was as though the Duke of Chetnole had risen from the dead. This was a time to celebrate the fact he was still alive and plan for the future.

But even as he settled in the green leather armchair and accepted a cigar, he couldn't shake off the feeling it was all because of Jenny. He lived because of her, her medicine, her care. For a moment, just a few days, all he had wanted to do was live for her. Live with her.

And now all that was over.

As it should be, Moses thought bitterly. *You'd be pulling that woman into a life so dark, so miserable, you'd crush her. She's happy in her cottage in the middle of nowhere, tending to the poor.*

Happier than she would have been with you? a cruel voice asked.

Moses pushed it aside. He couldn't think like that. He wouldn't.

"So," said Gilroyd, leaning back and puffing for a moment on his cigar. "I must say, Chetnole, it's a relief to see you. We were starting to think we'd have to give it all up entirely."

Moses shrugged. "I am sorry to have caused so much consternation."

"Consternation is the right word—panic for some, I think," Gilroyd said warningly. "Sedley is beside himself. Wincham will be delighted you've been found, and Penshaw will claim the credit for himself, as usual."

Moses inclined his head. "As usual."

"The whole of London was up in arms to think one of their brave and handsome dukes—their words, mind you—was missing, and in service to the Crown against the Frenchies."

"It wasn't quite like that," Moses said quietly.

Though what it was, he hardly knew. How could he tell Gilroyd, after everything the man had suffered, that he'd been distracted from returning to complete his mission, whatever it had been, because of a woman?

"We'd assumed you were dead," Gilroyd said steadily.

Moses tried to smile. Perhaps he was. There was certainly a dull, dead ache somewhere near his heart that did not seem to move, no matter what he thought or did. He'd wondered if the bath would help, but he still felt just as empty.

"You don't look well."

"I've . . . I've not been well," admitted Moses quietly, the cigar still in his hand unlit.

Gilroyd grunted. "Spot of stomach trouble?"

"Spot of getting stabbed in the back."

Gilroyd's eyes widened. "Dear God, I hope it isn't catching."

It was impossible not to laugh. "I don't think so, it was while I was in France. I think."

That was what he remembered, at any rate. But there was so much he did not. Why had he decided to leave France? It had been imperative—he recalled the sense of urgency driving him forward. But why?

There was plenty now that he wished to forget, too, but couldn't. The way Jenny smiled when she'd successfully seen to another patient. The joy in her eyes when she managed to untangle a medical mystery. The flutter of her eyelashes when he kissed—

"You know, for a dead man walking, you don't look very cheerful."

Moses blinked. Gilroyd was looking wary, as though being stabbed in the back truly was contagious.

What must they think of him? Missing for weeks, then suddenly turning up at old Gilroyd's house of all places. Why not go back to his own?

Because, Moses's battered mind tried to point out, *because you have spent too many daydreams thinking about taking Jenny there, that's why. And now you're back in London without her. You'll be without her for the rest of your life, and you can't bear to accept that.*

"I won't accept that."

"What's that?" asked Gilroyd suspiciously.

Moses's cheeks flamed with heat. *Had he really said that aloud?* "Nothing. Nothing, I just—I can't recall everything from the last few months. You'll have to forgive me."

Gilroyd's eyes widened as he reached to the table beside him, poured out a glass of whiskey, and thrust it in Moses's direction. "Fever with the stab wound?"

Moses nodded, accepting the drink. The liquor burned his throat, but it was a welcome pain. At least it couldn't hurt him for long.

"Ah. That would explain it, then. Your absence, I mean."

"I know I was coming back for a purpose," Moses muttered, half to himself. "I had to get back, and swiftly. I needed to . . . to tell someone something . . ."

Perhaps it was being back in Gilroyd's company, but it felt as though there were more memories resurfacing. Well . . . not memories exactly. Moses wouldn't call them anything that clear cut. More like . . . a sense of what he had been thinking at the time.

At the time when he had been stabbed in the back.

"There's a traitor," he said slowly.

The chair scraped as Gilroyd rose hurriedly. "What did you say?"

"It's just a feeling—a feeling that I knew that, that's why I was coming back to England," Moses said hastily, words spilling over each other. "I can't tell you more than that, but—"

"A traitor? Serving the Crown?" Gilroyd said urgently.

Panic was filling Moses's lungs, but the words felt true. *Had he said them? Thought them? Was that why he had returned to England so hurriedly?*

"I think so," he said quietly.

Moses met Gilroyd's gaze, and he saw something he had not expected. A lack of surprise.

"You knew," Moses breathed.

"Suspected," said Gilroyd, waving a hand as he sank back into his chair. "Too many things were getting out. Information only Snee and we dukes serving the Crown should know."

Moses stared, hardly able to take it in.

A traitor in their midst? One of their own, deciding to share information with the French—with their enemy? It didn't bear thinking about. But if it was the reason he had rushed back to England, and Gilroyd already suspected—

"Who was it?"

Moses blinked. Gilroyd's expression was urgent, his fist tight around his whiskey glass. "Who was—"

"That must have been why you came to England without orders," Gilroyd glared. "There can be no other reason—you must have discovered who it was! Damn it, man, you were literally stabbed in the back!"

Moses's mind raced but try as he might, he could not bring back memories from that time. It was like trying to recall a childhood dream. One might remember the shape of it, the sense of joy or fear it gave. But the details? The meaning, if there were any?

"I . . . I'm sorry," he said helplessly. "I cannot remember."

Gilroyd grunted. "Figures. Well, where have you been all this time, you with your injured shoulder and lack of memory. Find a doctor?"

Moses discovered to his horror there was a knot in his throat, making it impossible to speak. He found the best, the most beautiful, the cleverest—

"Spit it out man!" barked Gilroyd. "It's not as though you've got anything to be ashamed of. Not playing house with a woman after all, were you?"

He laughed. His laughter faded as Moses refused to meet his eye. He wouldn't admit—

"Dear God, you were! I jested about it with Sedley, and he told me off soundly," Gilroyd said with a sigh. "A woman? Dear God, you don't mean to tell me—"

"It wasn't like that," Moses said curtly.

"And to think, we were all worried sick!" continued Gilroyd forcefully. "If you're not careful, we'll start to think you are the trait—"

"Say that again and face me across a field with pistols, Gilroyd!" Moses had somehow found himself on his feet, a fist raised and a glare in his eye.

Gilroyd beheld him calmly for a moment, then grinned. "There's the Chetnole I know. Come on then, old friend. We've spent too long together and buried too many bodies to keep secrets. Spill."

Moses sat down heavily and dropped his head into his hands. "I don't know if I can. It's all so—she was so . . ."

He was a blackguard, a cruel man indeed, to bring up such a topic as this.

Try as he might, Moses could not stop himself from glancing over to the fireplace. Above it hung a painting. A painting of a man he knew well, the exact image of the man before him. And beside him in the painting . . .

A woman. Dark hair, laughing eyes, and a serious expression.

"Oh, God, man, just because I'm a widower, doesn't mean you have to censor yourself about the ladies," came Gilroyd's gruff voice.

Moses winced to hear him speak so harshly. "When Louisa was alive, you said—"

"I know what I said. You think I haven't committed every conversation with or about her to heart?" Gilroyd's voice was cold, distant. "We're not talking about my wife. We're talking about your . . . your whatever-she-was. What was she?"

"Just . . . just a woman."

Moses wasn't about to reveal all. Gilroyd wouldn't understand. Ever since his wife had died, since that terrible accident in which Louisa had lost her life, Gilroyd had not been the man to speak to about matters of the heart.

Not that he could blame him. Why, if he had lost Jenny . . .

Hadn't he already?

Gilroyd was laughing bitterly. "Well then, if she's just a woman it doesn't seem as though you left your heart behind in wherever you were. Good thing you didn't fall in love! That could have been fatal."

Moses swallowed. He was in love. He loved her. Jenny was

everything he could have wanted and more besides. But he had done the right thing. She could never have been happy slotting into his life, and he certainly could not have remained in East Langdon.

It was better this way. Even if everything in him ached, and he couldn't understand why nothing made sense, and—

"Dear God, man, you did fall in love."

Moses's head jerked up. "No, I—"

"There's no point in denying it, I've seen that look before," Gilroyd said heavily.

Now that was interesting. "Where?"

"In the looking glass," said Gilroyd, a morose smile creeping across his lips. "It's the look of a man who knows the woman he loves is far from his reach. That he's lost something precious and pure and is unlikely to find again. A man who is broken."

Broken. Yes, that described him rather well. And there was only one person who could put him back together, and she was the very reason he was shattered.

Cause and cure.

"Well, I'm afraid you'll have to forget her," Gilroyd said, sipping his whiskey. "I presume you couldn't bring her with you?"

Moses did not say anything. He just shook his head.

He couldn't even bring himself to say her name. Lady Genevieve Cotton-Powell may be a member of Society, but his Jenny had just been a woman. A beautiful, talented, bold woman who had taken great strides to create a life she wanted to live.

And he hadn't asked her to leave it. He wouldn't be so cruel.

"A woman like that is best left in the past—"

"You don't know her!" Moses found himself saying, glaring. "You didn't—no one could understand how brilliant, how impressive—"

"I am sure she was very nice," Gilroyd said, his smile fading. "But—"

"Nice?" No word could quite capture Jenny, but "nice" was

the absolute last thing Moses would have suggested. "Sometimes she's arrogant, and she's so sure she's right all the time—and the worst of it is, most of the time, she is right! And she's beautiful, Gilroyd, so beautiful. And kind. And she hates people—"

"Hates people?" repeated Gilroyd, confusion spread across his face.

"—and she cares for them too. There's a complexity to her I've never found in—"

"You think you're the only one to ever love a complex woman?" Gilroyd growled.

And just like that, all the passion died in Moses's throat. Damned right he wasn't the only one. He was sitting in a room with a man who knew, far better than anyone of his acquaintance, just what it was to love, and lose a love so precious as that.

Gilroyd sighed. "Forgive me. I do not intend to diminish your pain."

"Nor I yours," Moses said stiffly. *Dear God, if he'd wed Jenny and then lost her less than two years later, he'd be far more bitter than Gilroyd.* "It's just . . . it was difficult. Leaving her behind."

She would have his letter. What had she thought when she'd read it? Would she understand? Would Jenny recognize the sacrifice he had made, that they were both making, to ensure they could both contribute to creating a better world?

"I need to return to France," Moses said firmly. "Get back to work."

Nothing else would help rid him of this terrible pain.

But for some reason, Gilroyd was shaking his head. "You didn't receive my letter?"

"Yes, but—"

"Chetnole, the whole country has seen your name and engraving splashed across every newspaper," he said gently. "For weeks. Your time as a spy? It's over."

Moses had known that. But to hear it spoken aloud by another was all the more difficult.

He swallowed back his disappointment. "Then . . . then I'll go and see Snee tomorrow, find out what I can—"

"Chetnole, you don't understand," said Gilroyd wearily. "You've become . . . I don't know, some sort of *homme célèbre*."

Moses's stomach dropped. "I beg your pardon?"

"You're one of the most notorious men in Europe right now. Anywhere you go, anything you do—it's going to be watched. I'm sorry, but you're a liability," said Gilroyd. "Best thing you can do is lie low in the country somewhere."

With Jenny.

The thought had risen, unbidden. Moses pushed it aside hastily. There was absolutely no possibility of—

"Go back to that woman of yours."

Moses stared. Surely Gilroyd could not have said . . .

"There is no other remedy for this pain you feel but her," Gilroyd said, shaking his head and leaning back in his chair. "Trust me. I know."

"But—but the traitor, the work that needs to be done—"

"You let those of us with no love in our lives worry about that," said Gilroyd. "You need to go back for—what was her name?"

Moses swallowed. "Jenny. And truth be told, Gilroyd, after leaving her the letter I wrote . . . I'm not sure I'll be welcomed back."

CHAPTER EIGHTEEN

14 October 1811

"THERE," JENNY SAID to herself in the oppressive silence of the workroom. "Done."

Had she ever noticed before just how quiet it was? How the silence seemed to hang from the ceiling along with the herbs? How it weighed on her shoulders, heavier than any basket? How it filled her ears, deadening even the possibility of sound, until she could have sworn she was underwater?

"Well, you wanted quiet and solitude," Jenny said in the emptiness of the room. "And now you have it."

Who was it who advised caution in wishing for a change in one's lot?

One of her governesses might have said it, now Jenny came to think about it. Or was it from one of Aesop's fables? Either way, she had always thought the idea ridiculous. Of course she would be cautious whatever she did, whatever she wished for—she was a cautious person.

But that had been before she had become a doctor. Before she had found joy in serving East Langdon. Before she had found a half-dead man with a knife wound in his back . . .

Jenny swallowed the tears she knew would come as she started to place the jars of salve she had just finished making into one of her cupboards.

There was nothing to be gained by thinking of him. Moses—the Duke of Chetnole had decided to leave her. That was all there was to it.

She was not going to beg, Jenny thought calmly. Yes, a letter addressed to the Duke of Chetnole and sent to London would probably find him, but what would she say? *Please, Moses, come back to me. My life feels empty without you. Every night I reach out for you . . .*

Jenny cleared her throat loudly. "Nonsense."

No one responded. There was no one in the workroom. In fact, there had even been far fewer patients than normal, given the time of year.

Worry flickered. Was it possible the tide had finally turned against her? She had always feared that it would. Disrespect, or even a lack of respect, she could tolerate. But outright distrust?

If that ever occurred, she would have to pack up her workroom, try to find another village out of the way where her mother and brother would never find her, and begin again.

Again, again, Jenny thought. *How many times would she have to remake her life before she could simply live it?*

Thankfully, a knock at her front door pulled her from such morose meanderings.

"You like being alone," Jenny reminded herself as she stepped into the corridor toward the front door. "You always did."

And she had. Until she had learned how to be alone with Moses, and then suddenly any day without him felt empty, as though she was not even living.

"Ah, Mr. Saunders," Jenny said as brightly as she could. *Well, it was hardly the man's fault, was it, that she was so unhappy?* "How pleasant to see you."

But she said the words with a sinking feeling. He had never been particularly welcoming, and it was his wife who had always stood by Jenny's remedies. But Mrs. Saunders was not here. It was Mr. Saunders who stood before her, and he did not look happy.

"You," he spat, as though it were a malediction.

Jenny's smile faltered, but she forced herself to remain calm. This was just a conversation in which a patient wished to air his frustration. It was not unheard of. Unpleasant, but not unheard of.

"Good morning, Mr. Saunders," she said, hoping this would mediate the situation. "I hope you and Mrs. Saunders are—"

"She's still sick," said Mr. Saunders menacingly. "Even after six months ago, when I used that sweet smelling poultice you gave me for her. Even after advising her to keep her feet up and the weight off her back."

Jenny hesitated. It was a difficult case. A third child in as many years, and Mrs. Saunders was not a strong woman. There were things she could do, and she had done them. But sometimes . . .

"There are limits to what a doctor can do," she said, as softly as she could manage. "I am glad to hear Mrs. Saunders is resting, but—"

"You said it would help!"

"I said it *should* help," reminded Jenny, far more kindly than the aggressive man warranted. "Mr. Saunders—"

"I thought you could help her!" said the man, distress seeping into his tones.

Once again, Jenny blinked back tears. He clearly was devoted to his wife, something many other men in the village could learn from. Mr. Saunders may be a prickly sort, and he may not be the most overtly romantic of men, but it was easy to see his affection for Mrs. Saunders and his desperation to see her well.

Both her and the child.

"Why don't I come and visit her tomorrow as part of my rounds?" Jenny suggested, reaching out to pat the man on the shoulder. "I am sure—"

"You can't be sure—how can you be? You're no doctor!"

snapped Mr. Saunders, jerking his shoulder away so she couldn't touch him. "You didn't even want to make her well. You, you—you *wanted* to make her sick!"

Just for a moment, Jenny closed her eyes and attempted to get her bearings. It was common, when a loved one was weakening, for panic to set in. She had to try to calm the poor man down.

"Mr. Saunders—"

"I don't want you coming anywhere near my wife or my children, do you hear me?" pressed on Mr. Saunders, seemingly oblivious to her good intentions. "You're no doctor, you're—you're a witch!"

And there it is, thought Jenny dully. *We think we've come a great way as a country, and perhaps in some areas we have. But the same old superstitions are alive and well. We still think salt must be thrown over the shoulder if spilled, we still hesitate to make a bargain on a full moon.*

And we still look at women who heal as witches.

"Mr. Saunders," she said determinedly. She had to get hold of this conversation. "You may be as unkind as you wish, but that is not true. All I have ever done is—"

"Old Mrs. Guernsey should never have sold this place to you!" Mr. Saunders continued, unwilling to let her speak. "And you are killing my wife. You're killing her!"

"Her third pregnancy in so short a time is killing her, Mr. Saunders, and I am doing everything in my power to save her!" Jenny said sharply. *Honestly, couldn't the man see?* "If you would just listen to me—Mr. Saunders!"

The last two words were gasped rather than spoken. It was rather difficult to speak when a man had you by the throat and had thrust you against your own front door.

"You listen to me," Mr. Saunders hissed, pain in his eyes, as Jenny's panic flared. "You—you're the reason she's sick, see? S-So if . . . if you're gone . . ."

Bright lights were popping in the corners of Jenny's eyes as her fingers scrabbled at his hands—but Mr. Saunders had working hands, farmer hands, and they were wide and strong and had her in such a grip she could not escape.

Jenny was a doctor. She knew what a lack of air did to a person. She had read about a lack of oxygen in *A Modern Examination of the Human Body and Its Many Complexities*. Oxygen deprivation was startlingly bad for the body, and not something she had ever wished to experience.

Now she understood, far better than before, the panic that rose in the chest, the tightening of the lungs, the lights springing in the corners of one eyes, and the dull dimness, the knowledge you would never breathe again. It was seeping into her mind, the certainty that this was it. She would die here at the hands of a man who could not accept that she had done her best. And all before she ever saw Moses again—

"Unhand her, you brute!"

A thump, a thud, a groan: all those sounds happened, though in what order, Jenny could not quite tell. All she knew was that the clasping hand around her throat had gone and she was on the ground, gasping for air.

Her vision was cloudy and her senses confused, but she was almost certain there was a fight of some sort happening around her.

A fight? Over her?

Jenny blinked and Mr. Saunders came back into view. He was standing feet away, his nose bloody and his hand tucked under one arm. And opposite him . . .

She had to blink again just to make sure she wasn't dreaming. Perhaps she was hallucinating, the lack of oxygen from Mr. Saunders's strong grip making it impossible to tell.

But her breathing was slowing now, her grateful lungs taking in enough air, and still Moses stood there.

His eye was red and starting to swell—it would soon be black and shiny—and his lip was cut. But it was still Moses. He was standing there, between herself and Mr. Saunders, and his shoulders were heaving thanks to his ragged breathing.

She was surely dreaming. Lack of air, after all, could have a most vexatious effect on the mind. And this would be precisely what she would dream up, wouldn't it? Moses Warwick, Duke of Chetnole, back to save her. Returned from wherever it was he went to escape her.

If only that could be true . . .

"Go home," Moses was saying curtly. "And we can forget this ever happened, Mr. Saunders."

"But—but the doctor! Doctor Powell, I'm sorry, I didn't mean to—"

"Just go," said Moses sinisterly. "And we'll never mention it again."

Footsteps. Jenny was trying to push herself up, but the lack of oxygen had had a significant effect. *Worth remembering,* her mind tried to say. *Useful to know how a patient feels, if she ever came across this again . . .*

"Jenny? Jenny?"

Jenny blinked. Moses was kneeling beside her, his eye looking far worse close up than it did when he was standing. "Moses? What are you—Moses!"

For a second time in just a few minutes—how many minutes had it been?—Jenny had gasped at the sudden movement of a man, but this time it was soft and gentle.

Moses carried her carefully into the workroom and placed her in an armchair. Jenny had tried not to think too much about his strong arms around her, the way she could breathe in his musky scent, the warmth of his chest. Now that all those things were gone, she missed them.

Not that she should get too attached now. Whatever Moses had come back for, he wouldn't stay long. His letter had been perfectly clear.

"Are you all right?" Moses said urgently, kneeling before her to look into her eyes. "He didn't hurt you? You look fine, but—"

"Are you the doctor now?" Jenny said wryly.

Moses flushed, then straightened up. "I just . . . I thought—"

"If you ask me, it's you that needs the doctor," she added, taking in the growing purpling around his eyes. "That's going to look terrible in the morning."

If he was still here in the morning. Though she had wished to say it, she just couldn't bring herself to say the words and then be contradicted.

Her pulse was racing, and Jenny knew her hopes were rising, despite all her efforts to keep them down.

He was here. Moses.

After reading his letter, she had been certain she would never see him again. Moses had decided to leave her, despite everything they had shared, and that was that. He was not the sort of man to second guess his decisions. He was hard pushed to second guess even his opinions.

Yet he was here. She could not be dreaming this, for how else would she have returned to her workroom?

Phrases from his letter swam into Jenny's mind, unbidden.

I cannot stay. Duty takes me forward, and though I still cannot remember why I decided to return to England from France, the fact is that I did. I must go on to London. I must serve my country, as you serve your little slice of England.

The words had stung, yes. But they had been true.

Yet despite it all . . . he was here.

"You protected me," Jenny said awkwardly.

Moses nodded. "I couldn't—I wouldn't let Mr. Saunders do that to any woman. Do that to any person, in truth. It's a barbaric way to behave."

Any woman. Well, she had hoped to know whether or not he was here for good. Now she had received her answer. He would have done it for anyone. She was not special.

"He's in great pain," Jenny said woodenly. "His wife—"

"Love shouldn't bring you to commit acts like that," Moses said. "Love should—it should lighten, brighten the world. Not bring darkness into it."

Try as she might, Jenny could not bring herself to look up

into Moses's eyes. Meeting his gaze would tear down all the walls she had so recently been forced to build around her heart to defend it.

How could he say that to her? How could he be here?

Moses winced, lifting a hand to his face. "Damn it—"

"I said it would hurt in the morning," Jenny said, unable to help herself.

"Yes, well, it hurts now," snapped Moses.

She swallowed. *And will I see you in the morning? Will I be here to see just how black that eye is? The visible evidence of how you rushed to protect me, giving no thought to the consequences or your own health?*

And did she want to?

"Come on," Jenny said quietly, rising to her feet.

Moses moved toward her. "You mustn't—"

"You let me be the judge of what I should and shouldn't do," said Jenny firmly. Besides, her head hardly swam now. "I've got some salve, ready-made, that will do wonders on that eye. Come on."

Trying not to give the tall, handsome man with whom she had shared everything another look, Jenny stepped over to the cupboard where just minutes ago she had placed the salve she had finished making that morning.

The jars were still warm.

"Sit there, by the window," Jenny ordered, not looking round. "I'll need the light."

Moses must have obeyed, for she could sense him moving across the workroom. It had always been that way since they had first made love. Maybe before. She was conscious of his presence even with her back turned. Something in her knew where he was.

Until he had left her.

"I don't need any more doctoring," Moses said gruffly as Jenny approached him with the salve.

She permitted herself a small smile. "The number of times I hear that."

He nodded, but only briefly. "Come on, then. Let's get

this . . . you put it on."

Jenny swallowed. *What had Moses been about to say—let's get this over with?* But then why had he returned at all, if it was only to leave her again? Why did he wish to hurt her with this sudden coming and going? Had the other words in his letter not been true?

I truly respect you, Jenny. I hope you will think as fondly of me as I will think of you.

Slowly, she unscrewed the lid of the jar and dipped a finger into the salve. It shook only slightly as she lifted it to Moses's face.

"Stay still," Jenny exhaled.

It was all she could do to speak at all. There was something strange humming between them, an almost audible thrum as Jenny reached out and stroked Moses's face.

Not stroked—soothed. No, *applied salve.*

That was it. She was a doctor, and in this moment, he was just her patient. Just a man who had got himself into a bit of a trouble and needing fixing up.

Slowly, trying not to think about the intimacy of this moment, Jenny smoothed her salve around Moses's black eye.

He winced again.

"I am sorry," said Jenny quietly. "I know it stings—"

"It's quite all right," Moses said stiffly. "I knew what I was getting into when I wrenched that blackguard off you. For a moment, I thought . . . you didn't seem to be . . ."

His throat worked, but no more words came.

She could say nothing. How could she put into words her relief, her gratitude, when it was mingled with pain and confusion at his sudden return? Jenny knew no words that could do her heart justice.

Her stomach swooped as Moses closed his eyes so she could apply the salve to the top of his eyelid. There was something so trusting about the way he meekly accepted her care. It was a world away from the angry man who had told her, in no uncertain terms, that she could not be a doctor.

"I . . . I am glad I was able to be of some service," said Moses curtly as he lifted his eyelids. "I-I was passing through, and—"

Jenny's affections were full, her lips trembling. "You . . . you came back."

Moses met her eye and she saw with astonishment that his were full of tears. "I should never have left."

And then somehow, Jenny did not know how, she was kissing him—kissing Moses as though she would never be afforded the chance to kiss him again. Gasping for him, breathing him in as though he were the very air she craved. And he was kissing her back, the jar of salve forgotten, all aches and pains gone, as they clung to each other.

His hands were around her, holding her tight, and Jenny could have wept at the possessiveness she felt within him. He wanted her. Though she could not understand why, he was back. And he would never leave again.

At least, not without her.

The kiss ended as abruptly as it had begun. Jenny pulled back, looking up into Moses's eyes, and asked the question she had to have answered before she could open up her heart once again.

"You said once," Jenny murmured, "a duke a day keeps the doctor away."

Moses groaned. "Never has a more false word been spoken."

"Then . . . then you're here for good?" she asked.

"For you," said Moses seriously, pushing back some of her curls which had escaped their pins in their fervor. "For you. Forever."

CHAPTER NINETEEN

23 October 1811

"Y OU ARE ABSOLUTELY certain?" asked Jenny sternly. "This is not negotiable, Moses."

Moses groaned. "Do you think I would have suggested it if I weren't?"

They were on another walk, along another lane, but this time they were far from Kent.

It had been remarkably difficult to extricate Lady Genevieve Cotton-Powell from Kent, as it turned out. Despite having only lived there for three years or so, Jenny had become very attached to the place and its people.

And Mr. Saunders's attack on her notwithstanding, the people of East Langdon had grown fond of her. Accustomed to her ways. Dependent on her medicine. And Jenny had turned up her nose at the idea of leaving at first.

That was when the negotiations had started.

"I have been informed a most suitable candidate can and will be found," Moses said with as much confidence as he could muster. "I even met with the man suggested by Walsingham himself."

Jenny shot him a glance as they strode arm in arm toward the village. "Doctor Walsingham? You met with him? What's he like?"

Like any man, really, Moses wanted to say. He did not quite understand the fascination his wife-to-be had with Walsingham. Moses had sent a note to the revered doctor, and the person who had arrived at the requested meeting appeared to be nothing more than a polite, well-educated, quiet doctor. And that was all.

"He was fine."

"Fine? Fine?" Jenny repeated, snorting as she looked ahead of them. "You met one of the greatest medical minds in the whole of England, and you thought he was fine?"

"I've already met one of the greatest medical minds in the whole of England," said Moses, gently nudging the woman he loved. "And I'm afraid Walsingham was nowhere near as good looking."

Clearly despite herself, Jenny grinned. "You are incorrigible you know, Moses."

"I should hope so," he said cheerfully as the lane broadened out and became the main street through Chetnole Wayleigh. "I'd hate to find a cure for *all* my bad habits."

Their mingled laughter filled the chilly air as frost still clung to the few leaves in the trees. The year was fast approaching its end, and another week would bring a very important day in Moses's life.

His stomach turned over as he thought about it.

His wedding day. Now that was something he had never given much thought to.

"I would appreciate Doctor Walsingham's recommendation," Jenny was saying. "East Langdon needs a doctor, and my leaving has been a terrible blow to the people there."

Moses shook his head ruefully. "They were so ungrateful to you, yet still you care for them."

"A doctor doesn't heal to receive thanks," she pointed out.

"Perhaps you should," Moses said severely.

In some ways, he did not think he would ever truly understand this caring nature Jenny possessed in spades.

He himself could not plow or mend, nor could he involve himself in any sort of industry for fear of losing his reputation in Society. Working as a spy had seemed the obvious course of action, and he had worked hard for honor, duty, responsibility, a sense of service to one's country. But he didn't do it because he was a good person. Heaven forbid.

Jenny, on the other hand . . .

"The real question is, have you tracked down the traitor?" Jenny asked, her voice suddenly serious. "Did you speak to Justice Snee? The magistrate?"

Moses sighed. "I did, and he is still none the wiser."

It had been a most frustrating meeting. After he had finally managed to coax Jenny out of her workroom, they returned to London, and Moses had been eager to meet with Gilroyd and Mr. Snee together upon his return. The three of them, surely, could root out this miscreant who had done so much damage.

Yet it appeared not. Despite all their efforts, despite Gilroyd carefully placing a few lies into the network and Mr. Snee liaising with those he knew in the north, nothing had come of it.

Moses frowned, despite the comfort of Jenny's hand in his arm. It was infuriating.

The traitor's name must be in his head somewhere, but for the life of him, he could not remember!

"Could there be someone who would betray their own country?" Jenny wondered as they meandered past Chetnole Wayleigh's village green. "It doesn't seem possible!"

"There are plenty of dark things a man will do for a little money or prestige," Moses said darkly. "Old Vaughn—Thornfalcone now, actually, since he came into a dukedom—"

"How precisely does one come into—"

"He worked for us for a while. With Chantmarle, mostly," Moses continued. Perhaps the less he said about this, the better. "And he liked to frequently remind us that every man had his price. A man could have all the principles in the world, and still, there would be something he would sacrifice everything for. All you had to do was find it out."

A chill settled in him. It was a disheartening thought, that every man could be bought in one way or another. But still, he could not deny the veracity of the man's words.

"And you?"

Moses blinked, looking down at the eyes of his beloved. "Me?"

"What would your price be?" Jenny asked quietly. "I suppose there is something you would sacrifice everything for."

"Someone."

Her cheeks reddened. "You don't mean—"

"Let's just say it's a good thing I left the life of a spy behind me just as I fell completely in love," Moses said with a laugh as they turned a corner and meandered down a lane scattered with little cottages. "I dread to think what I would do if you had been put in true danger and I was the only one who could rescue you."

It was a sobering thought. Gilroyd had always said—at least, ever since Louisa died—that being in love made you vulnerable. Made it possible for your most obvious weakness to be used against you.

For so long, Moses had not understood. Now he could see precisely what his friend meant.

"Probably a good thing you're retiring then."

Moses groaned. "Retiring? You make me sound like an old man!"

There was a smile dancing on Jenny's lips. "Well, you are— what? Two and thirty?"

"That is hardly old!" he said hotly. "Why, it's not even middle . . . you're laughing at me, aren't you?"

"You are so easy to tease," Jenny said airily. "I cannot help it."

"And I cannot help this," Moses replied, his voice darkening to a growl as he pushed Jenny off the path and against a fence post.

He'd held off from kissing her for too long. The ache of longing had been building all day—all week. And though they had tried, time and time again, to promise each other they would at least do one thing Society expected and hold back until the wedding—

"Kiss me," begged Jenny, clutching his greatcoat's lapels to bring him closer.

Moses moaned, dipping his head to claim her lips. There was something about being asked—or ordered, he could never quite tell which—by the woman he loved. Something in Jenny's way of speaking that elevated his attraction to a level he had never known before.

It was intoxicating. And it meant the Duke of Chetnole was kissing Lady Genevieve Cotton-Powell against a fence in the middle of the countryside, with no thought to the consequences.

"Moses . . ."

How could he think of anything else? Jenny was pushed up against him, just as eager for his caresses as he was to give them. Pleasure sparked through his bones, Moses's head was spinning, and his manhood—

"We h-have to stop," Jenny stammered, nuzzling her lips close, forehead pressed against his.

Moses had to take several breaths before he had enough air to speak. "Why?"

"Because," Jenny said, her voice a seductive whisper, "we said we wouldn't—"

"We said we wouldn't make love," Moses corrected her, his hands moving down her gown to cup her buttocks, groaning as she leaned into him. "This is just a kiss."

"It's never just a kiss with you."

"Good," murmured Moses, desperately trying to remember himself. *He was a duke! He couldn't go about displaying his affection like this!*

Yet stepping away from Jenny was a complete impossibility. Not when she was so eager—

"Because we are in a lane, and anyone could see—"

"Let them see," growled Moses, all sense leaving his mind as ardor crept in to replace it. "You'll be my wife in a few days, so what does it matter—"

"And because there's someone coming," said Jenny, a laugh lilting her voice. "And I'm almost certain they're a patient."

Now that got his attention.

Dropping his beloved with great regret, Moses tried to catch his breath as he straightened his greatcoat. Jenny's passion for him appeared to be just as great as, if not greater than, his own for her, but her Physician's Oath still called to her.

"A patient?"

The moment the words left his mouth, he heard a quiet shuffling noise coming nearer.

Moses turned and looked up the lane, toward the village, and groaned as an elderly man came into view. "You mean Mr. O'Brien?"

"If that is his name," said Jenny serenely, though her cheeks bore the flushed evidence of their kiss from only moments before. "How long has he walked like that?"

Moses groaned again. "You cannot honestly tell me that you are about to—"

"Hie there, sir," Jenny said, striding away from Moses with purpose and not a single look back. "May I speak with you?"

He did not immediately follow her. Jenny knew what she was doing, and she did not need any help from him. Besides, Moses was almost certain he would only get in the way.

Not only was he not a doctor, he mused with a smile, *but he was also their duke.* Most of the residents of Chetnole Wayleigh could be depended upon to lose all power of speech when faced with the Duke of Chetnole. Unfortunately.

And so it was only a few scattered words that drifted on the light breeze that Moses was able to catch from Jenny's conversation with Mr. O'Brien. But it was enough.

"—entirely the wrong height for you, sir," Jenny was saying, looking critically at the walking stick the elderly man was leaning on. "See, if it were just a few inches taller—"

"You're saying a taller stick could cure the pain in my hip, young lady?" Mr. O'Brien asked suspiciously. "Who are you?"

And that, Moses thought, was his moment to step in.

"Ah, Mr. O'Brien," he said grandly as he stepped forward and bowed low to the man, as was due his age. "I see you have met my intended bride."

As expected, the old man's eyes widened, and a look of horror spread across his face. "Your—my dear lady, if I had known, I would never have—"

"It is quite all right, I'm a doctor," said Jenny evenly. "And I think—"

"A doctor?" said Mr. O'Brien, bewildered. He turned to Moses. "Your Grace, did she say—"

"Yes, she's a doctor," said Moses. "As much as a lady can be in our country. And the lack of more female doctors is naturally a great outrage, and I hope we all live to see the day when ladies can be doctors just as easily as gentlemen," he added, seeing Jenny's glare.

Mr. O'Brien evidently was lost in this conversation, but he studied Jenny with a beady eye. "You truly think the pain in my hip would go if my stick were longer?"

"Just a few inches," said Jenny. "And the pain in your back, too."

The man gaped. "How did you know—"

"I am a doctor," Jenny repeated, pride pouring from every syllable.

And Moses could not blame her. She was something, someone to be treasured. It was always pleasant to see someone else marveling at her, just as he did.

Mr. O'Brien was shaking her hand. "Any help you can be to me, Miss . . ."

"Lady, actually," Jenny said awkwardly. "But I prefer Doctor."

Moses did not snort. *Of course she did.*

"Come up to Chetnole Lacey and we'll measure you for a proper stick and have it ordered from London," Jenny was saying, "whenever it is convenient for you."

Though it had not appeared possible for Mr. O'Brien's eyes to grow any wider, Moses was quite astonished to see they could.

"Up to Chetnole Lacey? London? Whenever it—"

"Thank you, Mr. O'Brien, for your time," said Moses hastily. This had got more than a little out of hand, and the old man looked positively agog. "Good day."

"Good—good day, Your—"

"Don't forget," said Jenny, calling over her shoulder as Moses took her arm and marched her away. "Whenever it is convenient for you!"

Moses could not pretend he was surprised. He had taken Jenny out of East Langdon, but there were parts of her character he simply could not remove, even if he had wanted to. And he most certainly did not want to.

"Why did you cut that conversation short?" Jenny asked, frowning.

His stomach lurched. He had disappointed Jenny. Oh, Moses knew it was impossible to avoid it entirely, though he had been doing all he could to put off that day. But he was not perfect.

Though now he came to think of it, writing her that letter, disappearing from East Langdon, and coming back days later with little to no apology . . . that had probably already given her a hint. If she even needed one.

"You do know you're going to be a duchess, don't you?" Moses said conversationally, trying to put his various shortcomings out of his mind. "You can't just—"

"Duchess is all very well," Jenny cut across him. "But doctor? That is something I earned."

Moses halted and looked deep into her eyes.

There was defiance in there, and determination. An absolute certainty she was right, and—and fear. Fear that he would not understand.

Jenny's gaze did not waver. "Is there a doctor in your village, Moses?"

He winced. "It's not my—"

"This village, then," Jenny amended. "Chetnole Wayleigh. Does it have a doctor?"

How was it possible, Moses thought in wonder, *that she was so predictable?*

"What, this village?" he said innocently.

Wind rustled in the trees above them as Jenny put her hands on her hips and frowned. "I take it the answer is no, then?"

Moses sighed. "If I admit there isn't a doctor here, what are you going to do about it?"

He knew the answer. He had known it the minute Gilroyd had told him to go back to Jenny, to build a life together. He knew a life with Jenny would not only mean living with Genevieve Warwick, Duchess of Chetnole—as she would soon be.

No. It also meant living with Doctor Jenny Powell.

"I would tell you there is a doctor in your village," Jenny said lightly.

Moses frowned. "No there—"

"Am I not standing here right now?" The brightness of her words was triumphant, and Moses had to hand it to her: she had played him perfectly.

Still, he knew what was expected of him. Any excuse to tease her.

Moses let out a deep groan. "You can't tell me you're going to marry me merely for my doctorless village!"

"Greater matches have been made for less," Jenny shot back, slipping her hand through his arm.

Allowing himself to be pulled forward, Moses had to admit she was right. "Does this mean I need to give over my smoking room to become a workroom?"

"You don't even like smoking, so don't pretend it would be that great a hardship," Jenny said cheerfully. "Though if you are in the mood for handing over a room in that ridiculously large house of yours—"

"It's not ridiculously large!"

"Any house with two ballrooms is too large," said Jenny sharply as they turned a corner and the magnificent mansion appeared in view. "See, it's huge!"

Moses could not argue with her. It was only now he had returned, after years of serving his country in London and in France, that he realized just how large the place was. Arguably too large . . .

"I thought I might have one of them."

He blinked. "One of what?"

Jenny frowned. "The ballrooms, of course!"

"You cannot mean to—"

"You're not using it, and it would make the beginnings of a marvelous hospital," Jenny said, eyes alight with excitement. "Just think of the good we could do! Patients from all around—"

"People, you mean—"

"—the medicines they require, and food, too. I told you, it's insufficient food that causes the greatest problems," she continued without pausing for breath. "I truly think if we could educate the people about the importance of—"

"Are you ever going to have any time for balls in my other ballroom?" teased Moses, pride pouring through his chest. *This woman. This woman!* "Or hosting dinners, or visiting friends, or card parties, or anything like that?"

Jenny met his eye. They may be different, but they had reached an understanding which warmed Moses's soul. "Absolutely not."

"Will you have time for your own wedding?" Moses jested. "I would hate for you to find something more important than—"

This time, she did not ask. Jenny just kissed him, her eager lips tugging pleasure from his as her hands cupped his cheeks.

Moses lost himself in the kiss, which was far too short.

"Our wedding is important," Jenny said seriously, kissing the corner of his mouth before embracing him. "I'll have time for it."

"Good."

He wasn't going to reveal how relieved he was to hear her say that. After his sudden disappearance, then reappearance back into Jenny's life, Moses knew he had some making up to do. It would be cruel indeed if Jenny realized before their wedding day that he was absolutely not worthy of her.

"You do know I'm proud of you, don't you?" Moses said, pushing her back and gazing deep into Jenny's eyes.

They were filled with tears—but her smile suggested a diagnosis of joy, rather than despair.

"Of course you are," Jenny said lightly. "I would expect nothing less."

EPILOGUE

1 November 1811

"YOU ARE AN idiot," Jenny said firmly with absolutely no remorse. "A complete fool. I don't know why I bother with you."

"Neither do I," moaned Moses, rolling over in bed to grin. "And yet here you are."

Here she was. *It was a remarkable thing,* Jenny mused as she was pulled into Moses's arms and softened in the warmth of his embrace. And today . . .

"You know, you really should have let me sleep," Moses groaned. "I feel exhausted."

Jenny quivered, reveling in the way her buttocks moving against his hips made the man whimper. "Then I suppose I should have just bedded you once, rolled over, and fallen asleep?"

Moses kissed her neck lightly as he tightened his grip. "No. But if I yawn all the way through the service—"

"You wouldn't dare!" She turned, loosening herself from his grip and looking stern. "Not today, of all days!"

"Oh, is today particularly important?" grinned Moses.

Jenny laughed, despite herself. "Only a little."

A person's own wedding day, after all, did not occur very

often.

And they had waited long enough. When everything had been agreed upon, Jenny had thought the first of November seemed rather a long time off. More than enough time to put things into motion. Almost too much time, in fact, to keep her hands off the man who made her feel . . . well, everything.

And yet here it was. The first of November, and if they were not careful, they'd be late.

"We're going to be late," Jenny murmured as Moses's kisses returned to her neck, his hands to her hips, pulling her closer—but this time, facing him.

"Who cares?" Moses whispered, breath hitching in his throat. "I don't care if I'm late . . ."

"And I suppose I'm meant to be," Jenny said, eagerly capturing his lips with hers and pressing a scalding kiss to them. "You can't have a wedding without the bride . . ."

Over an hour later, the two of them lay back in the large bed in the ducal bedchamber, panting heavily.

"Damn it, woman, you shouldn't be able to do that," Moses said in a ragged voice.

Jenny grinned. "Flexibility is crucial for future health."

"I think it's crucial for other things, now," he said. "God in his Heaven, we are late."

Her stomach swooped. "And my mother will be here soon."

They hadn't talked much about her family. Jenny's letter to the residence of the Earl of Armstrong had been replied to in a stiff hand and with stiff words, but it had been replied to. That was more than she had expected.

Her brother would meet her at the church, the short note said. But her mother would arrive at Chetnole Lacey an hour before the bride was supposed to depart for the church.

It probably wouldn't do for her mother to find her in bed with a duke . . .

"Oh, I forget to tell you," said Moses hastily as Jenny stepped out of bed and slipped on the gentleman's dressing gown she had brought with her from West Cottage. "Doctor Walsingham sent a note."

Jenny turned hastily as she reached the door. "He did?"

The most eminent doctor in all of London—at least, to those who knew their craft. There were few people who had as good an eye for patients as Doctor Walsingham.

Moses nodded. "He's sent a friend, a Doctor Payne, to East Langdon. Apparently your workroom is astonishing."

Jenny grinned. "Just like me, then."

His laughter followed her as she strode down the corridor to the bedchamber where she was supposed to be sleeping until their wedding night. Jenny had been most firm: she must have her own, completely separate bedchamber. If Moses wanted her to live in Chetnole Lacey before they were wed, that was the only solution. They could not have people talking!

The fact that she had at no point slept in that chamber was neither here nor there.

It was therefore a great surprise when Jenny stepped lightly into the freezing room—why light a fire for a room that was perpetually empty?—to see a figure standing by the window.

"Mother!" Jenny hastily tugged her dressing gown tightly around her. If her mother were to see what little clothing she was wearing . . .

But the Dowager Countess of Armstrong seemed to know precisely what Jenny had been doing, and she turned around with an irate glare. "Genevieve. Ah. I see."

Jenny's cheeks burned. "I—"

"You are running late, my girl," said the Dowager Countess in clipped tones. "I brought my lady's maid. She's in the dressing room waiting for you."

Biting her lip, Jenny nodded. "Th-Thank you."

What did you say to someone after three years of silence? After a raucous argument that ended in door slamming and estrangement? What did you say to your mother on your wedding day?

The Dowager Countess cracked a smile. "A duke. I didn't think you had it in you."

Jenny straightened up and pushed her shoulders back. *She was not the child her mother thought she was.* "I did."

"Yes. Yes, I can see that," said her mother quietly. "And when all this is over, all this nonsense—"

"My wedding day, you mean?"

"Yes, that," said the Dowager Countess, waving a hand. "When the dust has settled, and you're back from your honeymoon . . . I would like to hear all about it."

Jenny frowned. "About my honeymoon?"

She had never taken her mother to be the sort of person who would wish to hear about Italy, but—

"No, about being a doctor in that godforsaken Kentish village, all on your own," the Dowager Countess said fiercely. "I've spent enough time out of your life, Jen. I-I think it's time I stepped back into it."

Jenny did not know what made her do it. There had been no words of apology, no grand speeches. Her mother had not taken a step closer to her, nor succeeded in bridging the gap of three years in a few sentences.

But progress had been made. And healing had to start somewhere.

Rushing across the room with her arms open, Jenny was relieved to find her mother opened her own to welcome her into an embrace. Only then did she realize she could not have wed that day without her mother sobbing into a scrap of lace on the front pew.

"Now then, no tears," said the Dowager Countess, completely ignoring her own. "You need to get into your gown. We have a wedding to get to!"

And so they did. Later, Jenny could hardly recall some of the details. It had certainly been a long time since a lady's maid had done her hair precisely how Society deemed it fashionable— different now to when she had left the *ton*. There was also no pencil in it, which was very disorienting. The carriage ride was not long, and it seemed the work of a moment to deliver her to a church full of pealing bells and flowers and stares.

But when she stood opposite Moses Warwick, Duke of Chetnole, at the altar, Jenny did not see a snooty nobleman.

She saw a man who had lit candles with shaking fingers over the bleeding body of a child. A man who had cut wood for an old woman. A man who had faced his prejudices, come to terms with his assumptions, and apologized—eventually—when he was wrong.

And a man who kissed like the devil.

A man who was kind, Jenny thought as her pulse leaped at his smile. That was all she had wanted. And she had so much more beside.

The golden wedding ring felt heavy on her finger, and Jenny could not stop staring at it as they returned to Chetnole Lacey.

"I still think you should have been married from your brother's house," said Moses conversationally as the carriage rocked.

Jenny rolled her eyes.

"It's not becoming of a duchess to roll her eyes, you know," Moses quipped.

She rolled her eyes again for good measure. "Doctors do it all the time."

A duchess. It was not something Jenny had given much thought to, because the truth of the matter was, she found the idea rather disconcerting.

Growing up the daughter of an earl . . . well, one had a few assumptions about what life was going to be like. And usually those assumptions were right.

Being a duchess, however, was not something she had even considered until a few weeks ago. She had only spoken to a few of the wives of Moses's friends, and she had not yet had time to form strong enough acquaintances to ask the most important questions.

Such as, who curtseyed to whom when she was presented at

St. James's and there was a foreign princess there? And why precisely did she have to serve fish on Fridays? And how many lady's maids did one actually need? It seemed like it was meant to be several, but what was Jenny going to have them all doing?

"God, I love you."

Jenny flushed as she looked up and saw Moses's worshipful expression. "Good."

"I think you're meant to say that you love me too," said her husband with a grin.

"I suppose I should," said Jenny, with a sigh. "And I do. It's just . . . well, I'm not looking forward to—"

"This will be the shortest wedding reception in the history of weddings, I promise you," said Moses, correctly guessing at the source of the discomfort. "I know how you despise company."

"I don't despise—"

"You do after an hour. I think I'm the only person you can stomach that long," he pointed out as the carriage rattled along the drive and started to slow. "But never fear. I'll chivvy people out before the hour is up. You have my word."

That was all very well, Jenny could not help but thinking two hours later, *yet here they still were*. She knew Moses meant to keep to his word, for he would not have said it if he had not meant it. But it was simply far more difficult getting people to leave a wedding reception than he had predicted.

"Finally, the daughter of the late Earl of Armstrong, back in Society," declared Lady Romeril in a loud, resounding voice. "About time, too!"

"I heard she was living in a cottage! An actual cottage!" said someone Jenny did not recognize as she walked past.

"Nonsense!" Lady Romeril said imperiously. "She was in one of the Russian courts, wasn't she? I heard an archduke wished to marry her and quite right, too . . ."

Jenny stifled a smile as she managed to reach the other side of the room, reaching out for Moses as though for a port in a storm. The nonsense that some people came up with! The truth was far more dull. Perhaps that was why the rumors continued to grow.

"I am sorry," said Moses wretchedly, as they looked out at the crowd across Chetnole Lacey's ballroom. "I just don't know how to make them go away!"

But Jenny had not grown up to be the woman she was, in Society until just a few years ago, without learning a few things. "Come on."

It was easy enough. All you had to do, Jenny knew, was walk by someone with your eyes fixed just past them, as though you were responding to a wave from another. And then again. And again. And before you knew it, you had marched past all your wedding guests and emerged—

"I never thought I would be so happy to see my own hall," gasped Moses, slamming the door behind them. "My goodness, I do not recall inviting such a horde!"

"I think my mother probably has something to do with that," said Jenny ruefully. "She did ask to be permitted to add to the guest list when she replied to my letter. I don't know why I believed she would limit herself to a short list."

"Well, we're alone now," her husband said with a mischievous grin on his face. "And that means—Gilroyd, leaving so soon?"

It was only politeness that made him say that, Jenny was sure—but then as she watched Moses step away from her and toward the tall, dark man who was pulling on a greatcoat, she was surprised to see something like real friendship in the look that passed between them.

Though she did not approach, since the man—whoever he was—was likely as not a part of Moses's spying past, she could not help but overhear what they were speaking of.

"—truly cannot recall?"

"The memory is gone, I think," Moses was saying with a sigh. "I know I left France with a purpose, and it was important or else I would not have left. But what it was—"

"No matter," shrugged the man her husband had called Gilroyd. "We'll work it out, Snee and I. If I go to France at all."

"You should get married again," said Moses softly. "It's no good to hide yourself away and—"

"—don't know what you're talking—"

"Marriage is an excellent tonic," her husband said, clasping the man's arm in a friendly gesture.

Jenny smiled at Moses's voice, but she gasped as Mr. Gilroyd shrugged off her husband and glared for good measure.

"You know the vow I've taken—you know I'll never marry again," said the man forebodingly. "Go and enjoy your bride, Chetnole. I'll take over the real business of spying and danger."

And without another word he strode away, slamming the front door shut behind him.

Jenny stared. *Now what on earth was that all about?*

"Don't mind him," Moses said heavily as he returned to her side. "Bitter, and I can't blame him."

"Grief affects us all in different ways," Jenny said quietly.

She did not think what she had said was particularly impressive, but apparently it was. Moses stared as though she had become clairvoyant, his jaw slack, eyes wide.

Jenny grinned. "What, you don't think I can spot the signs? That is clearly a man in grief. His wife, I suppose."

"I suppose at some point I shall have to grow accustomed to you always astonishing me," he said with a grin. "I suppose you can diagnose almost anything at fifty paces, can't you?"

Not quite, she wanted to say. *She'd been quite confused at first, when the nausea had arrived. Although, now she came to think of it . . .*

Well, they were alone, weren't they? If her mother had her way, and she was threatening—that was, promising—to do so, they would be blessed with the Dowager Countess's presence on a long visit. So this might be the only chance she had for a while, with just the two of them.

"Well, I can tell you *my* diagnosis, if you want."

Moses's smile rapidly disappeared. "Your—you are not unwell, are you?"

"It's not a sickness, not as such," she conceded, twining her fingers with his, her heart singing to see him so instantly concerned. "It's a relatively common ailment, and I believe it will be cured completely within the year."

"Within the year—how can you be sure?" Moses looked truly distressed now. "And here you are, walking all about the place— within a year?"

"Oh, just under eight months," said Jenny, her stomach swooping at the very thought. "Probably less."

"And that's if you take the right medicine, is that right?" Moses sighed heavily and pulled a hand through his hair. "Well, I know I just took a vow to care for you in sickness and in health, but I didn't expect so soon—"

"I am with child, you silly thing," Jenny said fondly, kissing the man she loved on the corner of his mouth. "With a baby!"

For a moment, Moses merely stared as though she had just announced she had tired of doctoring and had decided to become Prime Minister. *Not*, thought Jenny, *that she would do a particularly bad job. She would certainly do a better job than the current incumbent . . .*

Moses swept her up in his arms with a whoop of delight. "Jenny!"

Dizziness threatened to overwhelm her. "Put me down!"

Her husband immediately complied. "With child, with—you are sure?"

"As sure as I can be," said Jenny, laughing. "Oh, Moses, you don't mind that we're starting to expand our family so soon?"

"Mind?" Moses kissed her hard on the mouth before pulling her back into his arms. "I know I quipped once that a duke a day kept the doctor away—"

"Not this doctor," Jenny said, holding onto him tight. "This doctor has found a duke that she never, ever wants to leave."

"And you never will," breathed Moses, kissing her passionately once more. "You're stuck with me forever."

About Emily E K Murdoch

If you love falling in love, then you've come to the right place.

I am a historian and writer and have a varied career to date: from examining medieval manuscripts to designing museum exhibitions, to working as a researcher for the BBC to working for the National Trust.

My books range from England 1050 to Texas 1848, and I can't wait for you to fall in love with my heroes and heroines!

Follow me on twitter and instagram @emilyekmurdoch, find me on facebook at facebook.com/theemilyekmurdoch, and read my blog at www.emilyekmurdoch.com.

www.ingramcontent.com/pod-product-compliance
Lightning Source LLC
Chambersburg PA
CBHW060403310726
48976CB00003B/931